"Come here." Giancarlo's voice was a rasp, thick and hot, and it moved through her like joy.

Paige obeyed him, and this time she was happy to do it. She walked toward him, reveling in the way her blood pounded through her and her skin seemed to shrink a size, too tight across her bones. Because he could call this revenge. He could talk about hatred and penance. But it was still the same thick madness that felt like a rope around her neck. It was still the same inexorable pull.

It was still *them*.

He took her mouth like he was already deep inside her. Like he was thrusting hard and driving them both toward that glimmering edge. It was more than wild, more than carnal. He bent her back over her own arms, pressing her breasts into the flat planes of his chest, and he simply possessed her with a ruthless sort of fury that set every part of her aflame.

She thrilled to his boldness, his shocking mastery. The glorious taste of him she'd pined for all these years. The sheer *rightness*.

Paige kissed him back desperately, deeply, forgetting about the games they played. Forgetting about penance, about trust. Forgetting her betrayal and his fury. She didn't care what he wanted from her, or how he planned to hurt her, or anything at all but this.

This.

Books by Caitlin Crews

Vows of Convenience

His for Revenge
His for a Price

Royal and Ruthless

A Royal Without Rules

Scandal in the Spotlight

No More Sweet Surrender
Heiress Behind the Headlines

Self-Made Millionaires

Katrakis's Last Mistress

Bride on Approval

Pure Princess, Bartered Bride

Undone by the Sultan's Touch
Not Just the Boss's Plaything
A Devil in Disguise
In Defiance of Duty
The Replacement Wife
Princess from the Past
Majesty, Mistress...Missing Heir

AT THE
COUNT'S BIDDING

BY
CAITLIN CREWS

First published in Great Britain 2015
by Mills & Boon, an imprint of Harlequin (UK) Limited,
Eton House, 18-24 Paradise Road, Richmond, Surrey, TW9 1SR

© 2015 Caitlin Crews

ISBN: 978-0-263-25752-6

Harlequin (UK) Limited's policy is to use papers that are natural, renewable and recyclable products and made from wood grown in sustainable forests. The logging and manufacturing processes conform to the legal environmental regulations of the country of origin.

Printed and bound in Great Britain
by CPI Antony Rowe, Chippenham, Wiltshire

AT THE
COUNT'S BIDDING

CHAPTER ONE

"I MUST BE hallucinating. And may God have mercy on you if I am not."

Paige Fielding hadn't heard that voice in ten years. It wrapped around her even as it sliced through her, making the breezy Southern California afternoon fade away. Making the email she'd been writing disappear from her mind in full. Making her forget what year it was, what day it was. Rocketing her right back into the murky, painful past.

That voice. *His voice.*

Uncompromisingly male. As imperious as it was incredulous. The faint hint of sex and Italy in his voice even with all that temper besides, and it rolled over Paige like a flattening heat. It pressed into her from behind, making her want to squirm in her seat. Or simply melt where she sat. Or come apart—easily and instantly—the way she always had at the sound of it.

She swiveled around in her chair in instant, unconscious obedience, knowing exactly who she'd see in the archway that led into the sprawling Bel Air mansion high in the Hollywood Hills called La Bellissima in honor of its famous owner, the screen legend Violet Sutherlin. She knew who it was, and still, something like a premonition washed over her and made her skin prickle in the scant seconds before her gaze found him there in the arched, open door, scowling at her with what looked like a healthy mix of contempt and pure, electric hatred.

Giancarlo Alessi. The only man she'd ever loved with every inch of her doomed and naive heart, however little good that had done either one of them. The only man who'd made her scream and sob and beg for more, until she was hoarse and mute with longing. The only man who still haunted her, and who she suspected always would, despite everything.

Because he was also the only man she'd ever betrayed. Thoroughly. Indisputably. Her stomach twisted hard, reminding her of what she'd done with a sick lurch. As if she'd forgotten. As if she ever could.

She hadn't thought she'd had a choice. But she doubted he'd appreciate that any more now than he had then.

"I can explain," she said. Too quickly, too nervously. She didn't remember pushing back from the table where she'd been sitting, doing her work out in the pretty sunshine as was her custom during the lazy afternoons, but she was standing then, somehow, feeling as unsteady on her own legs as she had in the chair. As lost in his dark, furious gaze as she'd been ten years ago.

"You can explain to security," he grated at her, each word a crisp slap. She felt red and obvious. Marked. As if he could see straight through her to that squalid past of hers that had ruined them both. "I don't care what you're doing here, Nicola. I want you gone."

She winced at that name. That hated name she hadn't used since the day she'd lost him. Hearing it again, after all this time and in that voice of his was physically upsetting. Deeply repellant. Her stomach twisted again, harder, and then knotted.

"I don't—" Paige didn't know what to say, how to say

it. How to explain what had happened since that awful day ten years ago when she'd sold him out and destroyed them both. What was there to say? She'd never told him the whole truth, when she could have. She'd never been able to bear the thought of him knowing how polluted she was or the kind of place, the kind of people, she'd come from. And they'd fallen in love so fast, their physical connection a white-hot explosion that had consumed them for those two short months they'd been together—there hadn't seemed to be any time to get to know each other. Not really. "I don't go by Nicola anymore."

He froze solid in the doorway, a kind of furious astonishment rolling over him and then out from him like a thunderclap, deafening and wild, echoing inside of her like a shout.

It hurt. It all hurt.

"I never—" This was terrible. Worse than she'd imagined, and she'd imagined it often. She felt an awful heat at the back of her eyes and a warning sort of ache between her breasts, as if a sob was gathering force and threatening to spill over, and she knew better than to let it out. She knew he wouldn't react well. She was lucky he was speaking to her at all now instead of having Violet's security guards toss her bodily from the estate without so much as a word. But she kept talking anyway, as if that might help. "It's my middle name, actually. It was a— my name is Paige."

"Curiously, Paige is also the name of my mother's personal assistant."

But she could tell by the way his voice grew ominously quiet that he knew. That he wasn't confused or asking her to explain herself. That he'd figured it out the moment he'd seen her—that she'd been the name on all those emails from his mother over the past few years.

And she could also tell exactly how he felt about that revelation. It was written into every stiffly furious line of his athletic form.

"Who cannot be you." He shifted and her breath caught, as if the movement of his perfect body was a blow. "Assure me, please, that you are no more than an unpleasant apparition from the darkest hour of my past. That you have not insinuated yourself into my family. Do it now and I might let you walk out of here without calling the police."

Ten years ago she'd have thought he was bluffing. *That* Giancarlo would no more have called the police on her than he would have thrown himself off the nearest bridge. But this was a different man. *This* was the Giancarlo she'd made, and she had no one to blame for that but herself.

Well. Almost no one. But there was no point bringing *her* mother into this, Paige knew. It was his he was concerned about—and besides, Paige hadn't spoken to her own in a decade.

"Yes," she said, and she felt shaky and vulnerable, as if it had only just occurred to her that her presence here was questionable, at best. "I've been working for Violet for almost three years now, but Giancarlo, you have to believe that I never—"

"Stai zitto."

And Paige didn't have to speak Italian to understand that harsh command, or the way he slashed his hand through the air, gruffly ordering her silence. She obeyed. What else could she do? And she watched him warily as if, at any moment, he might bare his fangs and sink them in her neck.

She'd deserve that, too.

Paige had always known this day would come. That this quiet new life she'd crafted for herself almost by accident was built on the shakiest of foundations and that all it would take was this man's reappearance to upend the whole of it. Giancarlo was Violet's son, her only child. The product of her fabled second marriage to an Italian count that the entire world had viewed as its own, personal, real-life fairy tale. Had Paige imagined this would end in any other manner? She'd been living on borrowed time from the moment she'd taken that interview and answered all the questions Violet's managers had asked in the way she'd known—thanks to her insider's take on Violet's actual life away from the cameras, courtesy of her brief, brilliant affair with Giancarlo all those years ago—would get her the job.

Some people might view that harshly, she was aware. Particularly Giancarlo himself. But she'd had good intentions. Surely that counted for something? *You know perfectly well that it doesn't,* the harsh voice in her head that was her last link to her mother grated at her. *You know exactly what intentions are worth.*

And it had been so long. She'd started to believe that this might never happen. That Giancarlo might stay in Europe forever, hidden away in the hills of Tuscany building his überprivate luxury hotel and associated cottages the way he had for the past decade, ever since she'd set him up and those sordid, intimate photographs had been splashed across every tabloid imaginable. She'd lulled herself into a false sense of security.

Because he was here now, and nothing was safe any longer, and yet all she wanted to do was lose herself in looking at him. Reacquainting herself with him. Reminding herself what she'd given up. What she'd ruined.

She'd seen pictures of him all over this house in the years she'd worked here. Always dark and forbiddingly elegant in his particularly sleek way, it took no more than a glance to understand Giancarlo was decidedly not American. Even ten years ago and despite having spent so much time in Los Angeles, he'd had that air. That *thing* about him that whispered that he was the product of long centuries of European blue bloods. It was something in the way he held himself, distant and disapproving, the hint of ancient places and old gods stamped into his aristocratic bones and lurking behind his cool dark gaze.

Paige had expected Giancarlo would still be attractive, of course, should she ever encounter him again. What she hadn't expected—or what she'd allowed herself to forget—was that he was so *raw.* Seeing him was like a hard, stunning blow to the side of her head, leaving her ears ringing and her heart thumping erratically inside her chest. As if he knew it, his head canted to one side as he regarded her, as if daring her to keep talking when he'd ordered her to stop.

But she couldn't seem to do anything but stare. As if the past decade had been one long slide of gray and here he was again, all of him in bold color and bright lights. So glaring and hot she could hardly bear to look at him. But she did. She couldn't help herself.

He stood as if he was used to accolades, or simply commanding the full and rapt attention of every room he entered. It was partly the clothes he wore, the fabrics fitting him so perfectly, almost reverently, in a manner Paige knew came only at astronomical expense. But it was more than that. His body was lean and powerful, a symphony of whipcord strength tightly leashed, the crackle of his temper and that blazing sensuality that felt like a touch from ten feet away, carnal and wild. Even though she knew he'd never willingly touch her again. He'd made that clear.

Giancarlo was still so beautiful, yes, but there was

something so *male* about him, so rampantly masculine, that it made Paige's throat go dry. It was worse now, ten years later. Much worse. He stood in the open doorway in a pair of dark trousers, boots, and the kind of jacket Paige associated with sexy Ducati motorcycles and mystical places a girl like her from a ramshackle desert town in Nowhere, Arizona, only fantasized about, like the Amalfi Coast. Yet somehow he looked as effortlessly refined as if he could walk straight into a black-tie gala as he was—or climb into a bed for a long, hot, blisteringly feral weekend of no-holds-barred sex.

But it did her no good to remember that kind of thing. For her body to ready itself for his possession as if it had been ten minutes since they'd last touched instead of ten years. As if it knew him, recognized him, wanted him— as deeply and irrevocably as she always had. As if *wanting him* was some kind of virus that had only ever been in remission, for which there was no cure.

The kind of virus that made her breasts heavy and her belly too taut and shivery at once. The kind of virus that made her wish she still danced the way she had in high school and those few years after, obsessively and constantly, as if that kind of extended, heedless movement might be the only way to survive it. *Him.* His marvelous mouth tightened as the silence dragged on and she sent up a prayer of thanks that he hadn't thought to remove his mirrored sunglasses yet. She didn't want to know what his dark gaze would feel like when she could actually see his eyes again. She didn't want to know what that would do to her now. She still remembered what it had been like that last time, that short and harsh conversation on the doorstep of her apartment building that final morning, where he'd confronted her with those pictures and had truly understood what she'd done to him. When he'd looked at her as if he'd only then, in that moment, seen her true face—and it had been evil.

Pull yourself together, she ordered herself fiercely. There was no going back. There were no do-overs. She knew that too well.

"I'm sorry," she managed to get out before he cut her off again. Before she melted into the tears she knew she'd cry later, in private. Before the loss and grief she'd pretended she was over for years now swamped her. "Giancarlo, I'm so sorry."

He went so rigid it was as if she'd slapped him, and yet she felt slapped. She hurt everywhere.

"I don't care why you're here." His voice was rough. A scrape that tore her open, ripping her right down her middle. "I don't care what game you're playing this time. You have five minutes to leave the premises."

But all Paige could hear was what swirled there beneath his words. Rage. Betrayal, as if it was new. Hot and furious, like a fire that still burned bright between them. And she was sick, she understood, because instead of being as frightened of that as she should have been, something in her rejoiced that he wasn't indifferent. After all this time.

"If you do not do this of your own accord," Giancarlo continued with a certain vicious deliberation, and she knew he *wanted* that to hurt her, "I will take great pleasure in dumping you on the other side of the gates myself."

"Giancarlo—" she began, trying to sound calm, though her hands nervously smoothed at the soft blouse and the pencil skirt she wore. And even though she couldn't see his eyes, she felt them there, tracing the curve of her hips and her legs beneath, as if she'd deliberately directed his gaze to parts of her body he'd once claimed he worshipped. Had she meant to do that? How could she not know?

But he interrupted her again.

"You may call me Count Alessi in the remaining four minutes before I kick you out of here," he told her harshly. "But if you know what's good for you, whatever name you're using and whatever con you're running today and have been running for years, I'd suggest you stay silent."

"I'm not running a con. I'm not—" Paige cut herself off, because this was all too complicated and she should have planned for this, shouldn't she? She should have figured out what to say to someone who had no reason on earth to listen to her. And who wouldn't believe a word she said even if he did. Why hadn't she prepared herself? "I know you don't want to hear a single thing I have to say, but none of this is what you think. It wasn't back then, either. Not really."

He seemed to *expand* then, like a great wave. As if the force of his temper soared out from him and crashed over the whole of the grand terrace, the sloping lawn, the canyons all around, the complicated mess of Los Angeles stretched out below. It crackled as it cascaded over her, making every hair on her body seem to stand on end. That mouth of his flattened and he swept his sunglasses from his face at last—which was not an improvement. Because his eyes were dark and hot and gleamed a commanding sort of gold, and as he fastened them on her he made no attempt at all to hide the blistering light of his fury.

It made her want to sit down, hard, before she fell. It made her worry her legs might give out. It made her want to cry the way she had ten years ago, so hard and so long she'd made herself sick, for all the good that had done. She felt dangerously, dizzyingly hollow.

"Enlighten me," he suggested, all silken threat and that humming sort of violence *right there* beneath his elegant surface. Or maybe not really *beneath* it, she thought, now that she could see his beautiful, terrible face in all its furious perfection. "Which part was not what I thought? The fact that you arranged to have photographs taken of us while we were having sex, though I am certain I told you how much I hated public exposure after a lifetime in the glare of my mother's spotlight? Or the fact that you sold those photos to the tabloids?" He took a step toward her; his hands were in fists at his side, and she didn't understand how she could simultaneously want to run for her life and run *toward* him. He was a suicide waiting to happen. She should know that better than anyone. "Or perhaps I am misunderstanding the fact that you have now infiltrated my mother's house to further prey on my family?" He shook his head. "What kind of monster *are* you?"

"Giancarlo—"

"I will tell you exactly what kind." His nostrils flared and she knew that look that flashed over his face then. She knew it far too well. It was stamped into her memories and it made her stomach heave with the same shame and regret. It made her flush with terrible heat. "You are a mercenary bitch and I believe I was perfectly clear about this ten years ago. I never, ever wanted to see your face again."

And Paige was running out of ways to rank which part of this was the worst part, but she couldn't argue. Not with any of what he'd said. Yet rather than making her shrink down and curl up into the fetal position right there on the terra-cotta pavers beneath their feet, the way she'd done the last time he'd looked at her like that and called her names she'd richly deserved, it made something else shiver into being inside her. Something that made her straighten instead of shrink. Something that gave her the strength to meet his terrible glare, to lift her chin despite all of that furious, condemning gold.

"I love her."

That hung there between them, stark and heavy. And, she realized belatedly, an echo of what she'd said ten years ago, when it had been much too late. When he'd believed her even less than he did now. When she'd known full well that saying it would only hurt him, and she'd done it anyway. *I'm so sorry, Giancarlo. I love you.*

"What did you say?" His voice was too quiet. So soft and deliberately menacing it made her shake inside, though she didn't give in to it. She forced her spine even straighter. "What did you *dare* say to me?"

"This has nothing to do with you." That was true, in its way. Paige wasn't a lunatic, no matter what he might think. She'd simply understood a long time ago that she'd lost him and it was irrevocable. She'd accepted it. This wasn't about getting him back. It was about paying a debt in the only way she could. "It never did have anything to do with you," she continued when she was certain the shaking inside her wouldn't bleed over into her voice. "Not the way you're thinking. Not really."

He shook his head slightly, as if he was reeling, and he muttered something in a stream of silken, shaken Italian that she shouldn't have felt like that, all over her skin. Because it wasn't a caress. It was its opposite.

"This is a nightmare." He returned his furious glare to her and it was harder. Fiercer. Gold fury and that darkness inside it. "But nightmares end. You keep on, all these years later. It was two short months and too many explicit pictures. I knew better than to trust a woman like you in the first place, but this ought to be behind me." His lips thinned. "Why won't you go away, Nicola?"

"Paige." She couldn't tolerate that name. Never again. It was the emblem of all the things she'd lost, all the terrible choices she'd been forced to make, all the sacrifices she'd made for someone so unworthy it made her mouth taste acrid now, like ash and regret. "I'd rather you call me nothing but *mercenary bitch* instead of that."

"I don't care what you call yourself." Not quite a shout. Not quite. But his voice thudded into her like a hail of bullets anyway, and she couldn't disguise the way she winced. "I want you gone. I want this poison of yours out of my life, away from my mother. It disgusts me that you've been here all this time without my knowing it. Like a malignant cancer hiding in plain sight."

And she should go. Paige knew she should. This was twisted and wrong and sick besides, no matter the purity of her intentions. All her rationalizations, all her excuses, what did any of them matter when she was standing here causing *more* pain to this man? He'd never deserved it. She really was a cancer, she thought. Her own mother had always thought so, too.

"I'm sorry," she said, yet again, and she heard the bleakness in her own voice that went far beyond an apology. And his dark, hot eyes were on hers. Demanding. Furious. Still broken, and she knew she'd done that. It stirred up sensations inside of her that felt too much like ghosts, an ache and a fire at once. But Paige held his gaze. "More than you'll ever know. But I can't leave Violet. I promised her."

Giancarlo's dark gaze blazed into a brilliant fury then, and it took every bit of backbone and bravado Paige had not to fall a step back when he advanced on her. Or to turn tail and start running the way she'd wanted to do since she'd heard his voice, down the expansive lawn, through the garden and out into the wild canyon below, as far as she could get from this man. She wanted to flee. She wanted to run and never stop running. The urge to do it beat in her blood.

But she hadn't done it ten years ago, when she should have, and from far scarier people than Giancarlo Alessi. She wouldn't do it now. No matter how hard her heart catapulted itself against her chest. No matter how great and painful the sobs she refused to let loose from inside.

"You seem to be under the impression I am playing a game with you," Giancarlo said softly, so very softly, the menace in it like his hand around her throat. What was the matter with her that the notion moved in her like a dark thrill instead of a threat? "I am not."

"I understand that this is difficult for you, and that it's unlikely you'll believe that was never my intention." Paige tried to sound conciliatory. She did. But she thought it came out sounding a whole lot more like panic, and panic was as useless as regret. She had no space for either. This was the life she'd made. This was what she'd sown. "But I'm afraid my loyalty is to your mother, not to you."

"I apologize." It was a snide snap, not an apology. "But the irony rendered me temporarily deaf. Did you—*you*—just utter the word *loyalty?*"

Paige gritted her teeth. She didn't bow her head. "You didn't hire me. She did."

"A point that will be moot if I kill you with my bare hands," he snarled at her, and she should have been afraid of him, but she wasn't. She had no doubt that he'd throw her off the estate, that if he could tear her to shreds with his words he would, and gladly, but he wouldn't hurt her. Not physically. Not Giancarlo.

Maybe that was the last remnant of the girl she'd been,

she thought then. That foolish, unbearably naive girl, who'd imagined that a bright and brand-new love could fix anything. That it was the only thing that mattered. She knew better now; she'd learned her lessons well and truly and in the harshest of ways, but she still believed Giancarlo was a good man. No matter what her betrayal had done to him.

"Yes," she said, and her voice was rough with all the emotion she knew she couldn't show him. He'd only hate her more. "But you won't."

"Please," he all but whispered, and she saw too much on his face then, the agony and the fury and the darkness between, "do not tell me you are so delusional as to imagine I wouldn't rip you apart if I could."

"Of course," she agreed, and it was hard to tell what hurt when everything did. When she was sure she would leave this encounter with visible bruises. "If you could. But that's not who you are."

"The man you thought you knew is dead, *Nicola,*" he said, that hated name a deliberate blow, and Paige finally did step back then, it was so brutal. "He died ten years ago and there will be no breathing him back to life with your sad tales of loyalty and your pretty little lies. There will be no resurrection. I might look like the man you knew, for two profoundly stupid months a lifetime ago, but mark my words. He is gone as if he never was."

It shouldn't be so sad, when it was nothing more than a simple truth. Not a surprise. Not a slap, even, despite his harsh tone. There was absolutely no reason she should feel swollen anew with all that useless, unwieldy, impossible grief, as if it had never faded, never so much as shifted an inch, in all this time. As if it had only been waiting to flatten her all over again.

"I accept both responsibility and blame for what happened ten years ago," she said as matter-of-factly as she could, and he would never know how hard that was. How exposed she felt, how off balance. Just as he would never know that those two months she'd lost herself in him had been the best of her life, worth whatever had come after. Worth anything, even this. "I can't do anything else. But I promised Violet I wouldn't leave her. Punish me if you have to, Giancarlo. Don't punish her."

Giancarlo Alessi was a man made almost entirely of faults, a fact he was all too familiar with after the bleakness of the past decade and the price he'd paid for his own foolishness, but he loved his mother. His complicated, grandiose, larger-than-life idol of a mother, who he knew adored him in her own, particular way. It didn't matter how many times Violet had sold him out for her own purposes—to combat tales of her crumbling marriage, to give the tabloids something to talk about other than her romantic life, to serve this or that career purpose over the years.

He'd come to accept that having one's private moments exposed to the public was par for the course when one was related to a Hollywood star of Violet's magnitude—which was why he had vowed never, ever to have children that she could use for her own ends. No happy grandchildren to grace magazine articles about her *surprising depths*. No babies she could coo over in front of carefully selected cameras to shore up her image when necessary. He'd never condemn a child of his to that life, no matter how much he might love Violet himself. He'd pass on his Italian title to a distant cousin of his father's and let the sharp brutality of all that Hollywood attention end with him.

He forgave his mother. It was who she was. It was *this* woman he wanted to hurt, not Violet.

This woman who could call herself any name she wanted, but who was still Nicola to him. The architect of his downfall. The agent of his deepest shame.

The too-pretty dancer he'd lost his head over like a thousand shameful clichés, staining his ancient title, his relationship with his late father, and himself in the process. The grasping, conniving creature who had led him around by his groin and made him a stranger to himself in the process. The woman who had made him complicit in the very thing he hated above all others: his presence in the damned tabloids, his most private life on parade.

He'd yet to forgive himself. He'd never planned on forgiving her.

Standing here in this house he'd vowed he'd never enter again, the woman he'd been determined he'd cut from his memory if it killed him within his reach once more, he told himself the edgy thing that surged in him, making him feel something like drunk—dangerously unsteady, a little too close to dizzy—was a cold, clear, measured hatred. No more and no less than she deserved.

It had to be cold. Controlled. He wouldn't permit it to be anything else. He wouldn't let it run hot, burn within him the way loving her had, take charge of him and ruin him anew. He wasn't that trusting, gullible fool any longer, not as he'd been then—so sure he'd been the experienced one, the calloused and jaded one, that no one could take advantage of. She'd made certain he'd never be that idiot again.

He would save that kind of heated, brooding dislike for the sprawling, sunbaked city of Los Angeles itself. For California, brown and gold with only its manufactured, moneyed swaths of green as relief in another breathless summer. For the elegant monstrosity that was La Bellissima. For his heedless, callow twenties playing silly playboy games with films and a parade of famous and beautiful lovers, which *this woman* had brought to a screeching, excruciatingly public halt. For that dry blast of relentless heat on the wind, spiced with smoke from far-off brushfires and the hint of the Pacific Ocean that never cooled it, that made him feel too edgy, too undone. For his mother's recklessness in lovers and husbands and assistants, in all her personal relationships to the endless delight of the predatory press, a trait of hers Giancarlo had long despaired of and had shared but once.

Once.

Once had been enough.

He studied Nicola—*Paige*—as she stood there before him, gazing back at him from her liar's eyes that were neither blue nor green, that fall of thick, dark hair with a hint of auburn that she'd tamed into a side plait falling over one bare, exquisitely formed shoulder. Back then her hair had been redder, longer. Less ink, more fire, and he wished he found the darker shade unpleasant, unattractive. She was still as tall as he remembered but had gone skinny in that way they all did here, as if the denial of every pleasure in the world might bring them the fame they wanted more than anything. More than breath, more than food. Much, much more than love, as he knew all too well.

Don't even think that word, he snarled at himself.

She stiffened as he let his gaze roam all over her, so he kept doing it, telling himself he didn't care what this woman, whatever the hell she called herself now, thought or felt. Because she'd made it clear that the only things she'd ever seen when she'd looked at him—no matter how many times he'd made her scream his name, no matter how many ways they'd torn each other up and turned each other inside out, no matter how deeply he'd fallen for her or how enthusiastically he'd upended his life for her in those two months they'd spent almost entirely in his bed—were Violet's fame and a paycheck to match.

It wasn't only his heart she'd broken. She'd ground his pride, his belief that he could read anyone's intentions at a glance and keep himself safe from the kind of grasping predators who teemed over this city like ants, under her heel. She'd completely altered the way he'd seen himself, who he was, as surely as if she'd severed one of his limbs.

Yet she still held herself well, which irritated him. She still had that dancer's easy grace and the supple muscle tone to match. He took in her small, high breasts beneath that sleeveless white shirt with the draped neck, then the efficient pencil skirt that clung to the swell of her hips, and his hands remembered the lush feel of both. The slick perfection of her curves beneath his palms, always such a marvel of femininity in such a lean frame. The exquisite way she fit in his hands and tasted against his tongue. She'd left her legs bare, toned and pretty, and all he could think about was the way she'd wrapped them around his hips or draped them over his shoulders while he'd thrust hard and deep inside of her.

Stop, a voice inside him ordered, *or you will shame yourself anew.*

Her disguise—if that was what it was—did nothing to hide her particular, unusual beauty. She'd never looked like all the other girls who'd flocked around him back then. It was that fire in her that had called to him from that first, stunning clash of glances across the set of the music video where they'd met. She'd been a backup dancer in formfitting tights and a sport bra. He'd been the high-and-mighty pseudo director who shouldn't have noticed her with a band full of pop stars hanging on his every word. And yet that single look had singed him alive.

He could still feel the same bright flames, even though she'd darkened her hair and wore sensible, professional clothes today that covered her mouthwatering midriff and failed to outline every last line of her thighs. Like the efficient secretary to his mother that he knew she'd proved herself to be over these past years, for some reason—and Giancarlo refused to let himself think about that. About her motives and intentions. Why she'd spent so long playing this game and why she'd bothered to excel in her position here while doing it. Why he couldn't look at her without wanting her, even with all of this time between them. Even knowing exactly what she'd done.

"Is this where you tell me your sob story?" he asked coldly, taking a grim pleasure in the way she reacted to his voice. That little jump, as if she couldn't control this crazy thing between them any more than he could. "There's always one in these situations, is there not? So many reasons. So many excuses."

"I'm not sobbing." He couldn't read that lovely oval of a face, with cheekbones made for a man to cradle between his palms and that wide mouth that begged to be tasted. Plundered. "And I don't think I've made any excuses. I only apologized. It's not the same thing."

"No." He let his gaze move over her mouth. That damned mouth. He could still feel the slide of it against his, or wrapped hot and warm around his hardness, trailing fire and oblivion wherever she used it. *And nothing but lies when she spoke.* "I'll have to see what I can do about that."

She actually sighed, as if he tried her patience, and he didn't know whether he wanted to laugh or throttle her. He remembered that, too. From before. When she'd

broken over his life like a hurricane and hadn't stopped
tearing up the trees and rearranging the earth until she
was gone the same way she'd come, leaving nothing but
scandal and the debris of her lies in her wake.

And yet she was still so pretty. He found that made
him angrier than the rest of it.

"Glaring ferociously at me isn't going to make me
cry," she said, and he wanted to *see things* in those chameleon eyes of hers. He wanted something, anything, to
get to her—but he knew better, didn't he? She hadn't simply destroyed him, this time. She'd targeted his mother
and she'd done it right under his nose. How could he
imagine she was anything but evil? "It only makes the
moment that much more uncomfortable." She inclined her
head slightly. "But if it makes you feel better, Giancarlo,
you should go right ahead and try."

He did laugh then. A short, humorless little sound.

"I am marveling at the sight of you," he said, sounding cruel to his own ears, but she didn't so much as blink.
"You deserve to look like the person you really are, not
the person you pretended you were." He felt his mouth
thin. "But I suppose this is Hollywood magic in action,
no? The nastiest, most narcissistic things wrapped up
tight in the prettiest packages. Of course you look as
good as you did then." He laughed softly, wanting it to
hurt. Wanting something he said or did to have *some* effect on her—which told him a bit more than he wanted
to know about his unresolved feelings about this woman.
"That's all you really have, is it not?"

CHAPTER TWO

GIANCARLO HAD FANCIED himself madly in love with her.

That was the thing he couldn't forgive, much less permit himself to forget, especially when she was *right here* before him once again. The scandal that had ruined his budding film career, that had cast that deep, dark shadow over what had been left of his intensely private, deeply proper father's life, that had made him question everything he'd thought he'd known about himself, that had made him finally leave this damned city and all its demons behind him within a day of the photos going live—that had been something a few shades worse than terrible and it remained a deep, indelible mark on Giancarlo's soul. But however he might have deplored it, he supposed he could have eventually understood a pampered, thoughtless young man's typical recklessness over a pretty girl. It was one of the oldest stories in the world.

It was his own parents' story, come to that.

It was the fact that he'd been so deceived that he'd wanted to *marry* this creature despite his lifelong aversion to the institution, make her his countess, bring her to his ancestral home in Italy—he, who had vowed he'd never marry after witnessing the fallout from his parents' tempestuous union—that made his blood boil even all these years later. He'd been plotting out weddings in his head while she'd been negotiating the price of his disgrace. The fury of it still made him feel much too close to wild.

She only inclined her head again, as if she was perfectly happy to accept any and all blame he heaped on her, and Giancarlo didn't understand why that made him even more enraged.

"Have you nothing to say?" he taunted her. "I don't believe it. You must have lost your touch in all these years, Nicola." He saw her jerk, as if she really did hate that name, and filed that away as ammunition. "I beg your pardon. *Paige.* You can call yourself whatever you want. You've obviously spent too much time with a lonely old woman if this is the best you can do."

"She *is* lonely," Paige agreed, and he thought that was temper that lit up her cheeks, staining them, though her voice was calm. "This was never meant to be a long-term situation, Giancarlo. I assumed you'd come home and recognize me within the month. Of course, that was three years ago."

It took him a moment to understand what it was he was feeling then, and he didn't like it when he did. *Shame.* Hot and new and unacceptable.

"The world will collide with the sun before I explain myself to you," he bit out. Like how he'd managed to let so much time slip by—always so busy, always a crisis on the estate in Italy, always *something*. How he'd avoided coming here and hurt his mother in the process. Those things might have been true—they were why he'd finally forced himself to come after an entire eighteen months without seeing Violet on one of her usual press junkets around the globe—but they certainly weren't *this* woman's business.

"I didn't ask you to explain anything." She lifted one

shoulder, still both delicate and toned, he was annoyed to notice, and then dropped it. "It's simply the truth."

"Please," he scoffed, and rubbed his hand over his face to keep from reacting like the animal he seemed to become in her presence. Ten years ago he'd thought that compulsion—that need—was passion. Fate. He knew better now. It was sheer, unadulterated madness. "Do not use words you cannot possibly know the meaning of. It only makes you look even more grasping and base than we both know you are already."

She blinked, then squared her shoulders, her chin rising as she held his gaze. "Do I have time to get a list of approved vocabulary words in what remains of my five minutes? Before you have me thrown over Violet's walls and onto the street?"

Giancarlo looked at her, the breeze playing in her inky dark hair with its auburn accents, the sun shifting through the vines that stretched lazily above them in a fragrant canopy, and understood with a painful surge of clarity that this was an opportunity. This woman had been like a dark, grim shadow stretching over his life, but that was over now. And he was so different from the man he'd been when she'd sunk her claws in him that he might as well have been a stranger.

She had never been the woman she'd convinced him she was. Because *that* woman, he had loved. *That* woman had been like a missing piece to his own soul that he'd never known he lacked and yet had recognized instantly the moment he'd seen her.

But that was nothing but a performance, a stern voice whispered in his head.

And this was the second act.

"Does my mother know that you are the woman who starred in all those photos a decade ago?" he asked, sounding almost idle, though he felt anything but. He slid his hands into his pockets and regarded her closely, noting how pale she went, and how her lips pressed hard together.

"Of course not," she whispered, and there was a part of him that wondered why she wanted so badly to maintain his mother's good opinion. Why should that matter? But he reminded himself this was the way she played her games. She was good—so good—at pretending to care. It was just another lie and this time, he'd be damned if he believed any part of it.

"Then this is what will happen." He said it calmly. Quietly. Because the shock of seeing her had finally faded and now there was only this. His revenge, served nice and cold all these years later. "I wouldn't want to trouble my mother with the truth about her favorite assistant yet. I don't think she'd like it."

"She would hate it, and me," Nicola—*Paige* threw at him. "But it would also break her heart. If that's your goal here, it's certainly an easy way to achieve it."

"Am I the villain in this scenario?" He laughed again, but this time, he really was amused, and he saw a complex wash of emotion move over her face. He didn't want to know why. He knew exactly what he did want, he reminded himself. His own back, in a way best suited to please him, for a change. This was merely the dance necessary to get it. "You must have become even more delusional than your presence here already suggests."

"Giancarlo—"

"You will resign and leave of your own volition. Today. Now."

She lifted her hands, which he saw were in tight fists, then dropped them back to her sides, and he admired the act. It almost looked real. "I can't do that."

"You will." He decided he was enjoying himself. He couldn't remember the last time that had happened. "This isn't a debate, *Paige*."

Her pretty face twisted into a convincing rendition of misery. "I can't."

"Because you haven't managed to rewrite her will to leave it all to you yet?" he asked drily. "Or are you swapping out all the art on the walls for fakes? I thought the Rembrandt looked a bit odd in the front hall, but I imagined it was the light."

"Because whatever you might think about me, and I'm not saying I don't understand why you think it," she rasped, "I care about her. And I don't mean this to be insulting, Giancarlo, but I'm all she has." Her eyes widened at the dark look he leveled at her, and she hurried on. "You haven't visited her in years. She's surrounded by acolytes and users the moment she steps off this property. I'm the only person she trusts."

"Again, the irony is nearly edible." He shrugged. "And you are wasting your breath. You should thank me for my mercy in letting you call this a resignation. If I were less benevolent, I'd have you arrested."

She held his gaze for a moment too long. "Don't make me call your bluff," she said quietly. "I doubt very much you want the scandal."

"Don't make me call *your* bluff," he hurled back at her. "Do you think I haven't looked for the woman who ruined my life over the years? Hoping against hope she'd be locked up in prison where she belongs?" He smiled thinly when she stiffened. "Nicola Fielding fell off the face of the planet after those pictures went viral. That suggests to me that you aren't any more keen to have history reveal itself in the tabloids than I am." He lifted his brows. "Stalemate, *cara*. If I were you, I'd start packing."

She took a deep breath and then let it out, long and slow, and there was no reason that should have bothered him the way it did, sneaking under his skin and making him feel edgy and annoyed, as if it was tangling up his intentions or bending the present into the past.

"I genuinely love Violet," she said, her eyes big and pleading on his, and he ignored the *tangling* because he knew he had her. He could all but taste it. "This might have started as a misguided attempt to reach you after you disappeared, I'll admit, but it stopped being that a long time ago. I don't want to hurt her. Please. There must be a way we can work this out."

He let himself enjoy the moment. Savor it.

This wasn't temper, hot and wild, making him act out his passions in different ways, the line between it and grief too finely drawn to tell the difference. Too much time had passed. There was too much water under that particular bridge.

And she should never have come here. She should never have involved his mother. She should never have risked this.

"Giancarlo," she said, the way she'd said it that bright and terrible morning a decade ago when he'd finally understood the truth about her—and had seen it in full color pictures splashed across the entirety of the goddamned planet. When he'd showed up at the apartment she'd never let him enter and had that short, awful, final conversation on her doorstep. Before he'd walked away from her and Los Angeles and all the rest of these Hollywood machinations he hated so deeply. Five painful minutes to end an entire phase of his life and so many of his dreams. "Please."

He closed the distance between them with a single step, then reached over to pull on the end of that dark, glossy hair of hers, watching the auburn sheen in it glow and shift in the light. He felt more than heard her quick intake of breath and he wanted her in a thousand ways. That hadn't dimmed.

It was time to indulge himself. He was certain that whatever her angle was, her self-interest would win out over self-preservation. Which meant he could work out what remained of his issues in the best way imaginable. Whatever else she was, she was supple. *He had her.*

"Oh, we can work it out," he murmured, shifting so he could smell the lotion she used on her soft skin, a hint of eucalyptus and something far darker. *Victory,* he thought. His, this time. "It requires only that you get beneath me. And stay there until I'm done with you."

She went still for a hot, searing moment.

"What did you say?"

"You heard me."

Her changeable eyes were blue with distress then, and he might have loathed himself for that if he hadn't known what a liar she was. And what an actress she could be when it suited her. So he only tugged on her plait again and watched her tipped-up face closely as comprehension moved across it, that same electric heat he felt inside him on its heels.

That, Giancarlo told himself, was why he would win this game this time. Because she couldn't control the heat between them any more than he could. And he was no longer fool enough to imagine that meant a damned thing. He knew it was a game, this time.

"I want to make sure I'm understanding you." She swallowed, hard, and he was certain she'd understood him just fine. "You want me to sleep with you to keep my job."

He smiled, and watched goose bumps rise on her

smooth skin. "I do. Often and enthusiastically. Wherever and however I choose."

"You can't be serious."

"I assure you, I am. But by all means, test me. See what happens."

Her lips trembled slightly and he admired it. It looked so real. But he was close enough to see the hard, needy press of her nipples against the silk of her blouse, and he knew better. He knew she was as helpless before this *thing* between them as he was. Maybe she always had been. Maybe that was why it had all got so confused—she'd chosen him because he was Hollywood royalty by virtue of his parents and thus made a good mark, but then there'd been all of *this* to complicate things. But he didn't want to sympathize with her. Not even at such a remove.

"Giancarlo…" He didn't interrupt her but she didn't finish anyway, and her words trailed off into the afternoon breeze. He saw her eyes fill with a wet heat and he had to hand it to her, she was still too good at this. She made it so *believable.*

But he would never believe her again, no matter the provocation. No matter how many tears she shed, or *almost* shed. No matter how convincingly she could make her lips tremble. This was Hollywood.

This time, he wouldn't be taken by surprise. He knew it was all an act from the start.

"Your choices are diminishing by the minute," he told her softly. It was a warning. And one of the last he'd give her. "Now you have but two. Leave now, knowing I will tell my mother exactly why you've left and how you've spent these past years deceiving her. It might break her heart, but that will be one more black mark on your soul, not mine. And I'd be very surprised if she didn't find some way to make you pay for it herself. She didn't become who she is by accident, you must realize. She's a great deal tougher than she looks."

"I know she is." Her gaze still shimmered with that heat, but none of it spilled over—and he reminded himself that was *acting talent,* not force of will. "And what's the second choice?"

He shrugged. "Stay. And do exactly as I tell you."

"Sexually." She threw that at him, her voice unsteady but her gaze direct. "You mean do as you tell me *sexually.*"

If she thought her directness would shame him into altering his course here, she was far stupider than he remembered. Giancarlo smiled.

"I mean do as I tell you, full stop." He indulged himself then, and touched her. He traced the remarkable line of her jaw, letting the sharp delight of it charge through his bones, then held her chin there, right where he could stare her down with all the ruthlessness he carried within him. "You will work for me, *Paige.* On your back. On your knees. At your desk. Whatever I want, whenever I want, however I want."

He could feel her shaking and he exulted in it.

"Why?" she whispered. "This is *me,* remember? Why would you want to…?"

Again, she couldn't finish, and he took pleasure in these signs of her weakness. These cracks in her slick, pretty armor. Giancarlo leaned in close and brushed his mouth over hers, a little hint of what was to come. A little test.

It was just as he remembered it.

All that fire, arcing in him and in her, too, from the shocked sound she made. All that misery. Shame and fury and ten years of that terrible longing. He'd never quite got past it, and this was why. This thrumming, pounding excitement that had only ever happened here, with her. This unmatched hunger. This beautiful lie that would not wreck him this time. Not this time.

He needed to work it all out on that delectable body she'd wielded like a weapon, enslaving him and destroying him before she'd finally got around to killing him, too. He needed to make her pay the price for her betrayal in the most intimate way possible. He needed to work out his goddamned issues in the very place they'd started, and then, only then, would he finally be free of her. It had only been two months back then. It would have burned out on its own—he was sure of it, but they hadn't had time. He wanted time to glut himself, because only then would he get past this.

Giancarlo had to believe that.

"I know exactly who you are," he told her then, and he didn't pretend he wasn't enjoying this. That now that the shock had passed, he wasn't thrilled she'd proved herself as deceitful as he remembered. That he wasn't looking forward to this in a way he hoped scared her straight down into her bones—because it should. "It's long past time you paid for what you did to me, and believe me when I tell you I have a very, very detailed memory."

"You'll regret it." Her voice was like gauze and had as much effect.

"I've already regretted you for a decade, *cara*," he growled. "What does it matter to me if I add a little more?"

He leaned in closer, felt her quiver against him and thrilled to it. To her, because he knew her true face this time. He knew *her*. There would be no losing himself. There would be no fanciful dreaming of marriage and happy-ever-afters in the Tuscan countryside, deep in all the sweet golden fields that were his heritage. There would only be penance. Hers. Hard, hot, bone-melting penance, until he was satisfied.

Which he anticipated might take some time.

"This doesn't make sense." Did she sound desperate or did he want her to? Giancarlo didn't care. "You hate me!"

"This isn't hate," he said, and his smile deepened. Darkened. "Let's be clear, shall we? This is revenge."

Paige thought he would leap on her the moment she agreed.

And of course she agreed, how could she do anything *but* agree when Violet Sutherlin had become the mother her own had been far too addicted and selfish and hateful to pretend to be? How could she walk away from that when Violet was therefore the only family she had left?

But Giancarlo had only smiled that hard, deeply disconcerting smile of his that had skittered over her skin like electricity.

Then he'd dropped his hand, stepped away from her and left her alone.

For days. Three days, in fact. Three long days and much longer nights.

Paige had to carry on as if everything was perfectly normal, doing her usual work for Violet and pretending to be as thrilled as the older woman was about the return of her prodigal son. She'd had to maintain her poise and professionalism, insofar as there *was* any professionalism in this particular sort of job that was as much about handling Violet's personal whims as anything else. She'd had to try not to give herself away every time she was in the same room with Giancarlo, when all she wanted to do was scream at him to end this tension—a tension *he* did not appear to feel, as he lounged about, swam laps in the pool and laughed with his mother.

And every night she locked herself into the little cottage down near the edge of the canyon that was her home on Violet's property and tortured herself until dawn.

It was as if her brain had recorded every single moment of every single encounter she'd ever had with Giancarlo and could play it all back in excruciating detail. Every touch. Every kiss. That slick, hard thrust of his possession. The sexy noise he'd made against her neck each time he'd come. The sobs echoing back from this or that wall that she knew were hers, while she writhed in mindless pleasure, his in every possible way.

By the morning of the fourth day she was a mess.

"Sleep well?" he asked in that taunting way of his, his dark brows rising high when he met her on the back steps on her way into the big house to start her day. Violet took her breakfast and the trades on a tray in her room each morning and she expected to see Paige there, too, before she was finished.

Giancarlo stood on the wide steps that led up to the terrace, not precisely blocking her way, but Paige didn't rate her chances for slipping past him, either. Had she not been lost in her own scorching world of regret and too many vivid memories as she'd walked up the hill from her cottage, she'd have seen him here, lying in wait. She'd have avoided him.

Would you? that sly voice inside her asked.

A smart woman would have left Los Angeles ten years ago, never to return to the scene of so much pain and betrayal and heartache. A smart woman certainly wouldn't have got herself tangled up with her ex-lover's mother, and even if she had, she would have rejected Giancarlo's devil's bargain outright. So Paige supposed that ship had sailed a long time ago.

"I slept like a baby," she replied, because her memories were her business.

"I take it you mean that in the literal sense," he said drily. "Up every two hours wailing down the walls and making life a misery, then?"

Paige gritted her teeth. He, of course, glowed with health and that irritating masculine vigor of his. He wore an athletic T-shirt in a technical fabric and a pair of running shorts, and was clearly headed out to get himself into even better shape on the surrounding trails that scored the mountains, if that were even possible. No wonder he maintained that lean, rangy body of his that appeared to scoff at the very notion of fat. She wished she could hate him. She wished that pounding thing in her chest, and much lower, was *hate*.

"I've never slept better in my life," she said staunchly.

Her mistake was that she'd drifted too close to him as she said it, as if he was a magnet and she was powerless to resist the pull. She remembered that, too. It had been like a tractor beam, that terrible compulsion. As if they were drawn together no matter what. Across the cavernous warehouse where she'd met him on that shoot. Across rooms, beds, showers. Wherever, whenever.

Ten years ago she'd thought that meant they were made for each other. She knew better now. Yet she still felt that draw.

Paige only flinched a little bit when he reached over and ran one of his elegant fingers in a soft crescent shape beneath her eye. It was such a gentle touch it made her head spin, especially when it was at such odds with that harsh look on his face, that ever-present gleam of furious gold in his gaze.

It took her one shaky breath, then another, to realize

he'd traced the dark circle beneath her eye. That it wasn't a caress at all.

It was an accusation.

"Liar," he murmured, as if he was reciting an old poem, and there was no reason it should feel like a sharp blade stuck hard beneath her ribs. "But I expect nothing else from you."

Bite your tongue, she ordered herself when she started to reply. Because she might have got herself into this mess, twice, but that didn't mean she had to make it worse. She poured her feelings into the way she looked at him, and one corner of that hard, uncompromising mouth of his kicked up. Resignation, she thought. If they'd been different people she might have called it a kind of rueful admiration.

But this was Giancarlo, who despised her.

"Be ready at eight," he told her gruffly.

"That could cover a multitude of sins." So much for her vow of silence. Paige smiled thinly when his brows edged higher. "Be ready for what?"

Giancarlo moved slightly then on the wide marble step, making her acutely aware of him. Of the width of his muscled shoulders, the long sweep of his chiseled torso. Of his strength, his heat. Reminding her how deadly he was, how skilled. How he'd been the only man she'd ever met, before or since, who had known exactly what buttons to push to turn her to jelly, and had. Again and again. He'd simply looked at her, everything else had disappeared and he'd known.

He still knew. She could see it in that heat that made his dark eyes gleam. She could feel it the way her body prickled with that same lick of fire, the way the worst of the flames tangled together deep in her belly.

She felt her breath desert her, and she thought she saw

the man she remembered in his dark gaze, the man as lost in this as she always had been, but it was gone almost at once as if it had never been. As if that had been nothing but wishful thinking on her part.

"Wear something I can get my hands under," he told her, and there was a cruel cast to his desperately sensual mouth then that should have made her want to cry—but that wasn't the sensation that tripped through her blood, making her feel dizzy with something she'd die before she'd call excitement.

And as if he knew that too, he smiled.

Then he left her there—trying to sort out all the conflicting sensations inside of her right there in the glare of another California summer morning, trying not to fall apart when she suspected that was what he wanted her to do—without a backward glance.

"I think he must be a terribly lonely man," Violet said.

They were sitting in one of the great legend's favorite rooms in this vast house, the sunny, book-lined and French-doored affair she called her office, located steps from her personal garden and festooned with her many awards.

Violet lounged back on the chaise she liked to sit on while tending to her empire—"because what, pray, is the point of being an international movie star if I can't conduct business on a chaise?" Violet had retorted when asked why by some interviewer or another during awards season some time back—with her eyes on the city that preened before her beneath the ever-blue California sky and sighed. She was no doubt perfectly aware of the way the gentle light caught the face she'd allowed age to encroach upon, if only slightly. She looked wise and gorgeous at once, her fine blond hair brushed back from her face and only hinting at her sixty-plus years, dressed in her preferred "at home" outfit of butter-soft jeans that had cost her a small fortune and a bespoke emerald-green blouse that played up the remarkable eyes only a keen observer would note were enhanced by cosmetics.

This was the star in her natural habitat.

Sitting in her usual place at the elegant French secretary on the far side of the room, her laptop open before her and all of Violet's cell phones in a row on the glossy wood surface in case any of them should ring, Paige frowned and named the very famous director they'd just been discussing.

"You think *he's* lonely?" she asked, startled.

Violet let out that trademark throaty laugh of hers that had been wowing audiences and bringing whole rooms to a standstill since she'd appeared in her first film in the seventies.

"No doubt he is," she said after a moment, "despite the parade of ever-younger starlets who he clearly doesn't realize make him look that much older and more decrepit, but I meant Giancarlo."

Of course she did.

"Is he?" Paige affected a vague tone. The sort of tone any employee would use when discussing the boss's son.

"He was a very lonely child," Violet said, in the same sort of curious, faraway voice she used when she was puzzling out a new character. "It is my single regret. His father and I loved each other wildly and often quite badly, and there was little room for anyone else."

Everyone knew the story, of course. The doomed love affair with its separations and heartbreaks. The tempestuous, often short-lived reunions. The fact they'd lived separately for years at a time with many rumored affairs, but had never divorced. Violet's bent head and flowing tears at the old count's funeral, her refusal to speak of him publicly afterward.

Possibly, Paige thought ruefully as she turned every last part of the story over in her head, she had studied that Hollywood fairy tale with a little more focus and attention than most.

"He doesn't seem particularly lonely," Paige said when she felt Violet's expectant gaze on her. She sat very still in her chair, aware that while a great movie star might *seem* to be too narcissistic to notice anyone but herself, the truth was that Violet was an excellent judge of character. She had to be, to inhabit so many. She read people the way others read street signs. Fidgeting would tell her much, much more than Paige wanted her to know. "He seems as if he's the sort of man who's used to being in complete and possibly ruthless control. Of everything."

The other woman's smile then seemed sad. "I agree. And I can't think of anything more lonely," she said softly. "Can you?"

And perhaps that conversation was how Paige found herself touching up what she could only call defensive eyeliner in the mirror in the small foyer of her cozy little cottage when she heard a heavy hand at her door at precisely eight o'clock that night.

She didn't bother to ask who it was. The cartwheels her stomach turned at the sound were identification enough.

Paige swung open the door and he was there, larger than life and infinitely more dangerous, looking aristocratic and lethal in one of the suits he favored that made him seem a far cry indeed from the more casual man she'd known before. *This* man looked as if he'd sooner spit nails than partake of the Californian pastime of surfing, much less lounge about like an affluent Malibu beach bum in torn jeans and no shirt. *This* man looked as forbidding and unreachable and haughtily blue-blooded as the Italian count he was.

Giancarlo stood on the path that led to her door and let his dark eyes sweep over her, from the high ponytail she'd fashioned to the heavy eye makeup she'd used because it was the only mask she thought he'd allow her to wear. His sensual mouth crooked slightly at that, as if he knew exactly what she'd been thinking when she'd lined her eyes so dramatically, and then moved lower. To the dress that hugged her breasts tight, with only delicate straps above, then cascaded all the way to the floor in a loose, flowing style that suggested the kind of casual elegance she'd imagined he'd require no matter where he planned to take her.

"Very good, *cara*," he said, and that wasn't quite *approval* she heard in his voice. It was much closer to *satisfaction,* and that distinction made her pulse short-circuit, then start to drum wildly. Erratically. "It appears you are capable of following simple instructions, when it suits you."

"Everyone can follow instructions when it suits them," she retorted despite the fact she'd spent hours cautioning herself not to engage with him, not to give him any further ammunition. Especially not when he called her that name—*cara*—he'd once told her he reserved for the many indistinguishable women who flung themselves at him. *Better that than "Nicola,"* she thought fiercely. "It's called survival."

"I can think of other things to call it," he murmured in that dark, silken way of his that hurt more for its insinuations than any directness would have. "But why start the night off with name-calling?" That crook of his mouth became harder, deadlier. "You'll need your strength, I suspect. Best to conserve it while you can."

He's only messing with you, she cautioned herself as she stepped through the door and delivered herself into his clutches, the way she'd promised him she would. *He wants to see if you'll really go through with this.*

So did she, she could admit, as she made a show of locking the front door, mostly to hide her nerves from that coolly assessing dark gaze of his. But it was done too fast, and then Giancarlo was urging her into a walk with that hand of his at the small of her back, and their history seemed particularly alive then in the velvety night that was still edged with deep blues as the summer evening took hold around them.

Everything felt perilous. Even her own breath.

He didn't speak. He handed her into the kind of low-slung sports car she should have expected he'd drive, and as he rounded the hood to lower himself into the driver's seat she could still feel his hand on that spot on her back, the heat of it pulsing into her skin like a brand, making the finest of tremors snake over her skin.

Paige didn't know what she expected as he got in and started to drive, guiding them out of Violet's high gates and higher into the hills. A restaurant so he could humiliate her in public? One of the dive motels that rented by the hour in the sketchier neighborhoods so he could treat her like the whore he believed she was? But it certainly wasn't the sharp turn he eventually took off the winding road that traced the top of the Santa Monica Mountains bisecting Los Angeles, bringing the powerful car to a stop in a shower of dirt right at the edge of a cliff. There was an old wooden railing, she noted in a sudden panic. But still.

"Get out," he said.

"I, uh, really don't want to," she said, and she heard the sheer terror in her own voice. He must have heard it too, because while his grim expression didn't alter, she thought she saw amusement in the dark eyes he fixed on her.

"I'm not going to throw you off the side of the mountain, however appealing the notion," he told her. "That would kill you almost instantly."

"It's the 'almost' part I'm worried about," she pointed out, sounding as nervous as she felt suddenly. "It encompasses a lot of screaming and sharp rocks."

"I want you to suffer, *Paige,*" he said softly, still with that emphasis on her name, as if it was another lie. "Remember that."

It told her all manner of things about herself she'd have preferred not knowing that she found that some kind of comfort. She could have walked away, ten years ago or three days ago, and she hadn't. He'd been the one to leave. He'd hurled his accusations at her, she'd told him she loved him and he'd walked away—from her and from his entire life here. This was the bed she'd made, wasn't it?

So she climbed from the car when he did, and then followed him over to that rail, wary and worried. Giancarlo didn't look at her. He stared out at the ferocious sparkle, the chaos of light that was this city. It was dark where they stood, no streetlamps to relieve the night sky and almost supernaturally quiet so high in the hills, but she could see the intent look on his face in the reflected sheen of the mad city below, and it made her shake down deep inside.

"Come here."

She didn't want to do that either, but she'd promised to obey him, so Paige trusted that this was about shaming her, not hurting her—at least not physically—and drifted closer. She shuddered when he looped an arm around her neck and pulled her hard against the rock-hard wall of his chest. The world seemed to spin and lights flashed, but that was only the beaming headlights of a passing car.

Giancarlo stroked his fingers down the side of her face, then traced the seam of her lips.

Everything was hot. Too hot. He was still as hard and male as she remembered, and his torso was like a brand beside her, the arm over her shoulders deliciously heavy, and she felt that same old fire explode inside of her again, as if this was new. As if this was the first time he'd touched her.

He didn't order her to open her mouth but she did anyway at the insistent movement, and then he thrust his thumb inside. It was hotter than it should have been, sexy and strange at once, and his dark eyes glittered as they met hers with all of Los Angeles at their feet.

"Remind me how exactly it was I lost my head over you," he told her, all that fury and vengeance in his voice, challenging her to defy him. "Use your tongue."

Paige didn't know what demon it was that rose in her then, some painful mixture of long lost hopes and current regrets, not to mention that anger she tried to hide because it was unlikely to help her here, but she did as she was told. She grabbed his invading hand with both of hers and she worshipped his thumb as if it were another part of his anatomy entirely, and she didn't break away from him while she did it.

She didn't know how long it went on.

His eyes were darker than the night around them, and the same hectic gold lit them, even as it burned within her. She felt molten and wild, reckless and lost, and none of that mattered, because she could taste *him*. He might hate her, he might want nothing more than to hurt her, but Paige had never thought she'd taste him again. She'd never dreamed this could happen.

She told herself it didn't matter, those things she felt deep inside her that she didn't want to acknowledge. Only that this was a gift. It didn't matter what else it was.

He pulled his thumb out then and shifted her so they were facing each other, and the space between them seemed dense. Electric.

"I'm glad to see you haven't lost your touch," he said, and though his tone was cruel his voice was rougher than it had been, and she told herself that meant something. It meant the same thing her breathlessness did, or that manic tightening deep in her belly, that restlessness she'd only ever felt with him and knew only he could cure.

He smiled, and it was so beautiful it made her throat feel tight, and she should have known better. Because he wasn't finished.

"Get on your knees, *Paige*," he ordered her. "And do it right."

CHAPTER THREE

For a moment Paige thought she really had pitched over the side of the hill, and this taut, terrible noise in her head was her own scream. But she blinked and she was still standing there before Giancarlo, he was still waiting and she didn't want him to repeat himself.

She could see from that faintly mocking lift to his dark brows and that twist to his lips that he knew full well she'd heard him.

"Not *here*, surely," she said, and her voice sounded thin and faraway.

"Where I want. How I want. Was I unclear?"

"But I—" She cleared her throat. "I mean, I don't—"

"You appear to be confused." His hands were still on her, and that didn't help. The offhanded sweep of his thumbs against the tender skin of her bare shoulders made her want to scream, but she didn't think she'd stop if she started. "*I* this, *I* that. This isn't about you. This is about me."

"Giancarlo."

"I told you what to do," he said coolly. "And what will happen if you don't."

She jerked back out of his grip, furious in a sudden jolt, and not only because she knew he could have held her there if he liked. But because he hated her and she hated that he did. Because he was back in her life but not really, not in the way she'd refused to admit to herself she'd wanted him to be.

God, in those first months, those first years, she'd expected him to appear, hadn't she? She'd expected him to seek her out once his initial anger passed, once the last of the scandal had died down. To continue that conversation they'd had outside her apartment the morning the pictures had run, so swift and terrible. Because they might have been together only a short time, but he'd known her better than anyone else ever had. *Or ever would.* Maybe not the details of her life, because she'd never wanted anyone to know those, but the truth of her heart. She'd been so sure that somehow, he'd understand that there had to have been extenuating circumstances....

But he'd never come.

So perhaps it was a very old grief that added to the fury and made her forget herself completely.

"Is this really what you want?" she demanded, forgetting to hold her tongue, the taste of his skin still a rich sort of wine in her mouth, making her feel something like drunk. "Is this what a decade did to you, Giancarlo?"

"This is what you did to me." He didn't use that name then, but she was sure they could both hear it, *Nicola* hanging in the air and weaving in and out of the scent of the night-blooming jasmine and rosemary all around them. "And this is exactly what I want."

"To force me. To make me do things I don't want to do. To—" She found she couldn't say it. Not to the man who was the reason she knew that love could be beautiful instead of dark and twisted and sick. Not to the man who had made her feel so alive, so powerful, so perfect beneath his touch. "There are words, you know. Terrible words."

"None of which apply." He thrust his hands in the pockets of that suit, and she wondered if he found it hard to keep them to himself. Was she as sick as he was if that made her feel better instead of worse? How could she tell anymore—what was the barometer? "You don't *have* to do anything. I have no desire to force you. Quite the opposite."

"You told me I had to do this—to—to—"

"Don't stutter like the vestal virgin we both know you are not," he said silkily, and she wondered if he'd forgotten that she'd been exactly that when she'd come to him ten years ago. If he thought that was another lie. "I told you that you had to obey me. In and out of bed."

"That I had to have sex with you *at your command* or leave," she gritted out.

He didn't quite shrug, or smile. "Yes."

"So then I do, in fact, have to do something. You *are* perfectly happy to use force."

"Not at all." He shrugged as if he didn't care what happened next, but there was a tension to those muscled shoulders, around his eyes, that told her otherwise. And it wasn't in the least bit comforting. "You're welcome to leave. To say no at any time and go about your life, such as it is, using whatever name appeals to you. I won't stop you."

It was as if her heart was in her mouth and she felt dizzy again, but she couldn't look away from that terrible face of his, so sensual and impassive and cruel.

"But if I do that, you'll tell Violet who I am. You'll tell her I...what? Stalked you? Deliberately hunted her down and befriended her to get to you?"

"I will." His face hardened and his voice did, too. "It has the added benefit of being the truth."

But Paige knew better, however little she could seem

to express it to him. She knew what had grown between her and Violet in these past years, and how deeply it would wound the other woman to learn that Paige was yet one more leech. One more user, trying to suck Violet dry for her own purposes. It made her feel sick to imagine it.

"That's no choice at all."

"It's a choice, *Paige*," he said with lethal bite. "You don't like it, perhaps, but that doesn't make it any less of a choice, which is a good deal more than you offered me."

"I can't hurt her. Don't you care about that? *Shouldn't* you?"

"There are consequences to the choices you make," he said with a certain ruthless patience. "Don't you understand yet? This is a lesson. It's not supposed to be fun." That smile of his was a sharp blade she was certain drew blood. "For you."

For a moment she thought she'd bolt, though it was a long walk to anywhere from high up on this hill. She didn't know how she kept herself still, how she stayed in one piece. She didn't know how she wasn't already in a thousand shattered bits all over this little pull out on the side of the deserted road, like a busted-out car window.

"Tell me, then," she managed after a moment, keeping her head high, though her eyes burned, "how does this lesson plan work, exactly? You say you don't want to force me, but you're okay with me forcing myself? When it's the last thing I want?"

"Is it?" He shook his head at her, that smile of his no less painful. "Surely you must realize how little patience I have for lies, *Paige*." He let out a small sound that was too lethal to be a laugh. "If I were to lift your dress and stroke my way inside your panties, what would I find? Disinterest?"

Damn him.

"That's not the point. That's biology, which isn't the same thing as will."

"Are you wet?"

It wasn't really a question, and her silence answered it anyway. Her bright red cheeks that she was sure were like a flare against the night. A beacon. Her shame and fury and agony, and none of that mattered because she was molten between her legs, too hot and too slippery, and he knew it.

He knew it by looking at her, and she didn't know which one of them she hated more then. Only that she was caught tight in the grip of this thing and she had no idea how either one of them could survive it. How anything could survive it.

"Please," she said. It was a whisper. She hardly knew she spoke.

And the worst part was that she had no idea what she was asking for.

"We'll get to the begging," he promised her.

Giancarlo looked as ruthless as she'd ever seen him then, and it only made that pulsing wet heat worse. It made her ache and hunger and *want*, and what the hell did that make her? *Exactly what he thinks you are already,* a voice inside her answered.

And he wasn't finished. "But first, I want you on your knees. Right here. Right now. Don't make me tell you again."

He didn't think she'd do it.

They stood together in the dark, close enough that any observer would think them lovers a scant inch away from a touch, and Giancarlo realized in a sudden flash that he didn't want her to do it—that there was a part of him that wanted her to refuse. To walk away from this thing before it consumed them both whole and then wrecked them all over again.

To stop him, because he didn't think he could—or would—stop himself.

Seeing her had taken the brakes off whatever passed for his self-control and he was careening down the side of a too-steep mountain now, heedless and reckless, and he didn't care what he destroyed on the way down. He didn't care about anything but exploring the phrase *a pound of flesh* in every possible way he could.

She didn't blink. He didn't think either one of them breathed. He saw her clench her hands into fists, saw her stiffen her spine. He wanted to stop her from running. From not running. From whatever was about to happen next in this too-close, too-dark night, where the only thing that moved was that long dress of hers, rippling slightly against the faint breeze from the far-off sea.

Then she moved, in a simple slide of pure grace that was worse, somehow, than all the rest. It reminded him of so many things. The supple strength and flexibility of her body, her lean curves, and all the ways he'd worshipped her back before he'd known who she really was. With his hands. His mouth. His whole body. She was his memory in lovely action, a stark and pretty slap across his face, and when she was finished she was settled there on her knees before him.

Just as he'd asked. *Demanded.*

Giancarlo stared down at her, willing back all of his self-righteous fury and the armor it provided, but it was hard to remember much of anything when she was staring up at him, her eyes wide and mysterious and her lips slightly parted, making the carnal way she'd taken his thumb inside her mouth seem to explode through him all over again.

Making him realize he was kidding himself if he thought he was in control of this.

As long as *she* didn't realize that, Giancarlo thought, he'd manage. So he waited, watching her as he did. The night seemed much darker than it was, heavy on all sides and far fewer stars above than in the skies over his home in Tuscany, and he *felt* the ragged breath she took. That same old destructive need for her poured through him, rocketing through his veins and into his sex, making him clench his jaw too tight to keep from acting on it.

He felt like granite—everywhere—when she tilted herself forward and propped herself against his thighs, her palms like fire, her mouth much too close to the part of him that burned the hottest for her.

"Your mother thinks you're lonely," she said.

It took him a moment to understand the words she spoke in that husky tone of voice, and when he did, something he didn't care to identify coursed through him. He told himself it was yet more anger. He had an endless well where this woman was concerned, surely.

Giancarlo reached down and took her jaw in his hand, tugging her face up so he could look down into it, and it was the hardest thing he'd done in a long, long time to keep himself in check. In control. To crush the roaring thing that wanted only to *take her, possess her* and force himself to *think*, instead.

"That's not going to work," he told her softly. He was so hard it very nearly hurt, but he stood there as if he could do this all night, and he felt the faintest shiver move through her, making it all worthwhile.

"What do you mean? That's what she said."

"It doesn't matter if she hauled out her photo albums and wept over pictures of me as a fat, drooling infant," he said mildly, though his hand was hard against her jaw and he could feel how much she wanted to yank herself back, away from him. He could feel the flat press of her hands on his thighs, and the heat there that neither one of them had ever been any good at harnessing. "You're not bringing it up now, on your knees in the dirt because I ordered it, because you have a sudden interest in my emotional well-being."

"I could be interested in nothing *but* your emotional well-being and you'd tell me I was only running a con," Nicola—*Paige* said, with more bravado than he might have displayed were he the one kneeling there in the dark. "I don't know why I bother to speak."

"In this case," he said silkily, moving his hand along the sweet line of her jaw, her cheek, cradling her head with a softness completely belied by the lash in his words, "it is because you hope to shame me into stopping this. Why else bring up my mother when you're about to take me into your mouth at last?"

Her mouth fell open slightly more, as if in stunned astonishment, and he laughed, though it wasn't a very nice sound.

"Fine," she said, though her voice sounded like a stranger's. "Whatever you want."

"That is the point I am trying to make to you, *Paige,*" he bit out then, holding her immobile, so she had no choice but to gaze back at him, and he was a terrible man indeed, to revel in the temper he saw in her changeable eyes. "'Whatever I want' isn't an empty phrase. It could mean pleasuring me by the side of the road without any consultation whatsoever about your feelings on the subject. It is what *I* want. Are you beginning to understand me? How many object lessons do you think you will require before this sinks in?"

She said something in reply but the night stole her

words away, and she cleared her throat. She was trembling fully then, and he might have felt like the monster all that accusation in her gaze named him, but he could see the rest of it, too. The stain of color on her cheeks. That glassy heat in her eyes. And beneath the hand he still held to her face and against her neck, the wild drumming of her pulse, pounding out her arousal in an unmistakable beat.

He knew that rhythm better than he knew himself. He thought it might have been the only honest thing about her, then and now.

"How long?" she whispered.

"Until what?"

"Until this is done." She moistened her lips and he felt it like her wicked mouth, wet and soft and deep, and nearly groaned where he stood.

"Until I'm bored."

"A few hours, then," she said, with a remnant of her usual fire, and he smiled.

"I don't imagine you'll be that lucky." He traced a pattern from that stubborn chin of hers to the delicate shell of her ear, then back. "I've had a long time to think about all the ways I'd like to make you crawl. Then pay. Then crawl some more. There's no telling how long it could take."

"And yet when you had the chance, you talked to me for three seconds and then disappeared for a decade," she pointed out.

He felt that same wash of betrayal, that same kick in the gut he'd felt that long-ago day when he'd realized she'd used him the way his own mother always had—and it had been far more shattering, because Violet had only sold him out when he was clothed.

"I don't want to *talk* to you," he said, as harshly as he

could in that same soft voice. "I didn't then. I don't now. I thought I'd made that clear."

A car passed by on the winding mountain drive, the headlights dancing over them, and he saw something bleak in her eyes, across her lovely face. He told himself there was no echo at all inside him, no hollow thing in his chest.

"Then we'd better get started with the humiliation and sexual favors, hadn't we?" she said with a cheerfulness that was as pointed as it was feigned, and he felt her hands tighten against his thighs. She moved them up toward his belt and he didn't know he meant to stop her until he did.

He watched her face as he helped her rise to her feet, and he didn't let go of her arm when she was standing, the way he should have done.

"And here I thought we were right on target to get arrested for public indecency," she whispered, her voice still sharp but something raw in her chameleon gaze. "They could throw me in jail and charge me for solicitation and it would be like all your dreams come true in one evening."

"This is my dream," he growled at her, his hand wrapped tight around her arm and that fever in his blood. His revenge, he thought. At last. "It's not the act itself that matters, *cara.* That's a privilege you haven't earned. It's the surrender. It's all about the surrender." He laughed then, a dark sound he felt in every part of him, as if it was a part of the night and as dangerous, and then he let her go. It was harder than it should have been. "You'll learn."

It became clear to Paige in the week that followed that it wasn't Giancarlo's intention to *actually* make her have sex with him whenever and wherever he chose, no matter what provocative things he might say to the contrary.

That would have been easy, in its way. He was far more diabolical than that.

He wanted her in a constant state of panic, with no idea what he might do next. He wanted her to think of nothing at all but him and the little things he made her do to prove her obedience that were slowly driving her insane.

It's all about the surrender, he'd said. Her surrender. And she was learning what he'd meant.

One day—after nearly a week filled with anticipation and the faintest of touches, always in passing and always unexpected, all of which still felt like a metal collar around her neck that he tightened at will—he found her in Violet's expansive closet, putting together a selection of outfits with appropriate accessories for Violet to choose between for the event the star was scheduled to attend that evening.

"Pull up your skirt, take off your panties—if you are foolish enough to be wearing any—and hand them to me," Giancarlo said without preamble, making Paige jump and shiver into a bright red awareness of him, especially because her mind had been a long way away.

Ten years ago away, in fact, and treating her to a play-by-play, Technicolor and surround-sound replay of one of their more adventurous evenings in the Malibu house down on the beach she had no idea if he still owned.

"What?" she stammered out, but her body wasn't in any doubt about his instructions. Her breasts bloomed into an aching heaviness, making her bra feel too tight and too scratchy against her skin. Her stomach flipped over, and below, that shimmering heat became scalding.

And that was only at the sound of his voice. What would happen if he touched her this time?

"Is this your strategy, *cara*? To feign ignorance every time I speak to you?" He loomed in the doorway, looking untamed and edgy, furious and male. He'd forgone the exquisite suits and running apparel today and looked more like the Giancarlo she remembered in casual trousers and a top that was more like a devotional poem extolling the perfection of his torso than anything so prosaic as a *T-shirt*. "It's already tiresome."

She was standing too straight, too still, on the other side of the central island that housed Violet's extensive jewelry collection, entirely too aware that she resembled a deer stuck fast in the glare of oncoming headlights. But she couldn't seem to move.

Anything besides her mouth, that was. "I did try to warn you that this would get boring."

Giancarlo's mouth crooked slightly and made hers water. His eyes were so dark the gold in them felt as much like a caress as a warning, and she was terribly afraid she could no longer tell the difference.

"Show me that you know how to follow directions." He folded his arms over that chest of his and propped a shoulder against the doorjamb, but Paige wasn't the least bit fooled. He looked about as casual and relaxed as a predator three seconds before launching an attack. "And I'd think twice before making me wait, if I were you."

"It's all the threats," she grated at him. "They make me dizzy with fear. It's hard to hear the instructions over all the heart palpitations."

"I'm certain that's true." That crook in his mouth deepened. She was fascinated. "But I think we both know it isn't fear."

Paige couldn't really argue with that, and she certainly didn't want him to wander any closer and prove his point—did she? She glanced down at her outfit, the short, flirty little skirt with nothing on beneath it, and realized that she'd obeyed him without thinking about it when she'd dressed this morning. *Make sure that I have access to you, should I desire it,* he'd told her two nights ago, a harsh whisper in the hallway outside Violet's office. She'd obeyed him and in so doing, she'd revealed herself completely.

When she raised her gaze to his again, he was smiling, a fierce satisfaction in his dark gold eyes and stamped across that impossibly elegant face of his. He jerked his chin at her, wordlessly ordering her to show him, and her hands moved convulsively, as if her body wanted nothing more than to prove itself to him. To prove *herself* trustworthy again, to jump through any hoop he set before her—

But that wasn't where this was headed. This wasn't a love story. No matter how many memories she used to torture herself into imagining otherwise.

"Come over here and find out for yourself, if you want to know," she heard herself say. Suicidally.

Giancarlo only shook his head at her, as if saddened. "You seem to miss the point. Again. This is not a game that lovers play, *cara.* This is not some delightful entertainment en route to a blissful afternoon in bed. This is—"

"Penance," she finished for him, with far more bitterness than she should have allowed him to hear. "Punishment. I know."

"Then stop stalling. Show me."

Paige could see he meant it.

She told herself it didn't matter. That he'd seen all of her before, and in a far more intimate setting than this. That more than that, he'd had his mouth and his hands on every single inch of her skin, in ways so devastating and intense that she could still feel it ten years later. So what did it matter now? He was all the way across the room and he *wanted* her to balk. To hate him. That was why he was doing this, she was sure.

So instead, she laughed, like the carefree girl she'd never been. Paige stepped out from behind the center island so there could be no accusations of hiding. She watched his hard, hard face and then, slowly, she reached down and pulled her skirt up to her hips.

"Satisfied?" she asked when she was fully bared to his view—because she was.

She'd been so lost in her guilt, her shame, her own anger at everything that had happened and Giancarlo too, that she'd forgotten one very important fact about this thing between them that Giancarlo had been using to such great effect.

It ran both ways.

He stared at her—too hard and too long—and she saw the faintest hint of color high on those gorgeous cheeks of his. And that hectic glitter in his dark eyes that she recognized. Oh yes, she recognized it. She remembered it.

She knew as much about him as he did about her, after all. She knew every inch of *his* body. She knew his arousal when she saw it. She knew he'd be so hard he ached and that his control would be stretched to the breaking point. The chemistry between them wasn't only his to exploit.

She stood there with her skirt at her waist, supposedly debasing herself before the only man she'd ever loved, and Paige felt better than she had in years. Powerful. *Right*, somehow.

"Looked your fill?" she asked sweetly when the silence stretched on, taut and nearly humming. He swallowed as if it hurt him, and she felt like a goddess as he dragged his gaze back to hers.

"Come here." His voice was a rasp, thick and hot, and it moved in her like joy.

She obeyed him and this time, she was happy to do it. She walked toward him, reveling in the way her blood pounded through her and her skin seemed to shrink a size, too tight across her bones. Because he could call this revenge. He could talk about hatred and penance. But it was still the same thick madness that felt like a rope around her neck. It was still the same inexorable pull.

It was still *them*.

Paige stopped in front of him and let out a surprised breath when he moved, reaching down to gather her wrists in his big hands and then pull them behind her, securing them in one of his at the small of her back. Her skirt fell back into place against the sensitized skin of her thighs, her back arched almost of its own accord, and Giancarlo stared down at her, a hard wildness blazing from his eyes.

Paige remembered that, too.

She didn't know what he looked for, much less what he saw. He stared at her for a moment that dragged out to forever and she felt it like panic beneath the surface of her skin. Like an itch.

And then he jerked her close, her hands still held immobile behind her back, and slammed his mouth to hers.

It wasn't a brush of his mouth, a tease, like before. It wasn't an introduction.

He took her mouth as if he was already deep inside of her. As if he was thrusting hard and driving them both toward that glimmering edge. It was more than wild, more than carnal. He bent her back over her own arms, pressing her breasts into the flat planes of his chest, and he simply possessed her with a ruthless sort of fury that set every part of her aflame.

She thrilled to his boldness, his shocking mastery. The glorious taste of him she'd pined for all these years. The sheer *rightness.*

Paige kissed him back desperately, deeply, forgetting about the games they played. Forgetting about penance, about trust. Forgetting her betrayal and his fury. She didn't care what he wanted from her, or how he planned to hurt her, or anything at all but this.

This.

There was too much noise in her head and too much heat inside of her and she actually moaned in disappointment when he pulled back, holding her away from him with that iron strength of his that reminded her how gentle he was with it. How truly demanding, because he knew—as he'd always known—exactly what she wanted. How far away from *force* all of this really was.

"You kiss like a whore," he said, and she could see it was meant to be an insult, but it came out sounding somehow reverent, instead.

She laughed. "Have you kissed many whores, then? You, the exalted Count Alessi, who could surely have any proper woman he wished?"

"Just the one."

She should be wounded by that, Paige thought as she studied him. She should feel slapped down, put in her place, but she didn't. She cocked her head to one side and saw the fever in his dark gaze, and she knew that whatever power he had over her, she had it over him, too. And more, he was as aware of that as she was.

"Then how would you know?" she asked him, her voice like a stranger's, breathy and inviting. Nothing like hurt at all. "Maybe the whore is you."

"Watch your mouth." But he'd moved closer again, his shoulders filling her vision, her need expanding to swallow the whole world. Or maybe it was his need. Both of theirs, twined together and too big to fit beneath the sky.

"Make me," she dared him, and he muttered something in Italian.

And then he did.

He let go of her hands to take her face between his hard palms, holding her where he wanted her as he plundered her mouth. As he took and took and then took even more, as if there was no end and no beginning and only the madness of their mouths, slick and hot and perfect. The fire between them danced high and roared louder, and he didn't stop her when Paige melted against him. When she wound her arms around his neck and clung to him, kissing him back as if this was the reunion she'd always dreamed of. As if this was a solution, not another one of his clever little power games.

And she didn't know when it changed. When it stopped being about fury and started to taste like heat. When it started to feel like the people they'd been long ago, before everything had gone so wrong.

He felt it, too. She felt him stiffen, and then he thrust her aside.

And for a long moment they only stared at each other, both of them breathing too fast, too hard. Paige tried to step back and her legs wobbled, and Giancarlo scowled at her even as his hand shot out to steady her.

"Thank you," she said, because she couldn't help herself. Her mouth felt marked, soft and plundered, and Giancarlo was looking at her as if she was a ghost. "That certainly taught me my place. All that punitive kissing."

She didn't know what moved across his face then, but it scraped at her. It hurt far worse than any of his words had. She had to bite her own tongue to keep from making the small sound of pain that welled up in her at the sight of it.

"It will," he promised her, a bleakness in his voice that settled in her bones like a winter chill. Like the fate she'd been running from since the day she'd met him, loath as she was to admit it. "I can promise you that. Sooner or later, it will."

Kissing her had been a terrible mistake.

Giancarlo ran until he thought his lungs might burst and his legs might collapse beneath him, and it was useless. The Southern California sun was unforgiving, the blue sky harsh and high and cloudless, and he couldn't get her taste out of his mouth. He couldn't get the feel of her out of his skin.

It was exactly as it had been a decade ago, all over again, except this time he couldn't pretend he'd been blindsided. This time, he'd walked right into it. He'd been the one to kiss her.

He cursed himself in two languages and at last he stopped running, bending over to prop his hands on his knees and stare down the side of the mountain toward his mother's estate and the sprawl of the city below it in the shimmering heat of high summer. It was too hot here. It was too familiar.

Too dangerous.

It was much too tempting to simply forget himself, to pick up where he'd left off with her. With the woman who was no longer Nicola. As if she hadn't engineered his ruin, deliberately, ten years ago. As if she hadn't then tricked her way to her place at his mother's side with a new name and God only knew what agenda.

As if, were he to bury himself in her body the way he wanted to do more than was wise and more than he cared to admit to himself, she might transform into the woman she'd already proved she wasn't in the most spectacular way imaginable.

He was already slipping back into those old habits he'd thought he'd eradicated. The work he'd left in Italy was piling up high, and yet here he was, running off steam in the Bel Air hills the way he'd done when he was a sixteen-year-old. She was the first thing he thought of when he woke. She was what he dreamed about. She was taking over his life as surely as she ever had, very much as if this was *her* revenge, not his.

He was an addict. There was no other explanation for the state he was in, hard and ready and yearning, and he didn't want that. He wanted her humbled, brought low, destroyed. He wanted her to feel how he'd felt when he'd woken that terrible morning to find his naked body splashed everywhere for the entire world to pick over, parse, comment upon, like every other time his private life been exploited for Violet's gain—but much worse, because he hadn't seen the betrayal coming. He hadn't thought to brace himself for impact.

He wanted this to hurt.

Giancarlo straightened and shoved his hair back from his forehead, the past seeming to press against him too tightly. He remembered it all too well. Not just the affair with Nicola—*Paige,* he reminded himself darkly—in all its blistering, sensual perfection, as if their bodies had been created purely to drive each other wild. But the parts of that affair he'd preferred to pretend he didn't remember, all these years later. Like the way he'd always found himself smiling when they'd spoken on the phone, wide and hopeful and giddy, as if she was sunshine in a bottle and only his. Or the way his heart had always thudded hard when she'd entered a room, in the moment before she'd seen him and had treated him to that dazzling smile of hers that had blotted out the rest of the world. The way she'd held his hand as if that connection alone would save them both from darkness, or dragons, or something far worse.

Oh yes, he remembered.

And he remembered the aftermath, too. After the pictures ran in all those papers. After those final, horrible moments with this woman he had loved so deeply and known not at all. After he'd done the best he could to clear his head and then made his way back to Italy. To face, at last, his elderly father.

His father, who had felt denim was for commoners and had thought the only thing more tawdry than Europe's aristocracy was the British royals, with their divorces and dirty laundry and *jeans*. His father, Count Alessi, who could have taught propriety and manners to whole nunneries and probably had, in his day. His father, who had been as gentle and nobly well-meaning as he was blue-blooded. Truly the last of his kind.

"It is not your fault," he'd told Giancarlo that first night in the wake of the scandal. He'd hugged his errant son and greeted him warmly, his body so frail it had moved in Giancarlo like a winter wind, a herald of the coming season he hadn't wanted to face. Not then. Not yet. "When I married your mother I knew precisely who she was, Giancarlo. It was foolish to imagine she and I could raise a son untainted by that world. It was only a matter of time before something like this happened."

Perhaps his father's disappointment in him had cut all the deeper because it had been so matter-of-fact. Untouched by any hint of anger or vanity or sadness. There was nothing to fight against, and Giancarlo had understood that there had been no one to blame but himself for his poor judgment. His father might have been anti-quated, a relic of another time, but he'd instilled his values in his only son and heir.

Strive to do good no matter what, he'd told Giancarlo again and again. *Never make a spectacle of oneself. And avoid the base and the dishonorable, lest one become the same by association.*

Giancarlo had failed on all counts. It was why he knew that the vows he'd made when he was younger were solid. Right. No marriage, because how could he ever be certain that someone wanted *him*? And no heirs of his own, because he'd never, ever, subject a child to the things he'd survived. He might not be able to save himself from his own father's disappointment, he might find his life trotted out into public every time his mother starred in something new and needed to remind the world of her once upon an Italian count fairy-tale marriage, but it would end with him.

Damn Nicola—*Paige*—for making him think otherwise, even if it had only been for two mostly naked months a lifetime ago.

It was that, he thought as he broke into a run again, his pace harder and faster than before as he hurtled down the hill, that he found the most difficult to get past. He hated that she had betrayed him, yes. But far worse was this *thing* in him, dark and brooding, that yearned only for her surrender no matter how painful, and that he very much feared made him no different than she was.

He thought he hated that most of all.

CHAPTER FOUR

AFTER A LONG shower and the application of his own hand to the part of him that least listened to reason, Giancarlo prowled through the house, his fury at a dull simmer. An improvement, he was aware.

La Bellissima was the same as it ever was, as it had been throughout his life, he thought as he moved quietly through its hushed halls, gleaming with Violet's wealth and consequence in all its details. The glorious art she'd collected from all over the planet. The specially sourced artisan touches here and there that gave little hints of the true Violet Sutherlin, who had been born under another name and raised in bohemian Berkeley, California. Old Hollywood glamor mixed with contemporary charm, the house managed to feel light and airy rather than overfed, somehow, on its own affluence.

Much like Violet herself, all these years after her pouty, sex kitten beginnings in the mid-seventies. He should know, having been trotted out at key moments during her transition from kitten to lion of the industry, as a kind of proof, perhaps, that Violet could do more than wear a bikini.

There was the time she'd released a selection of cards he'd written her as a small child, filled with declarations of love that the other kids at school had teased him about all the way up until his high school graduation. There was the time she'd spent five minutes of her appearance in a famous actor's studio interview telling a long, involved anecdote about catching him and his first girlfriend in bed that had humiliated fourteen-year-old Giancarlo and made his then-girlfriend's parents remove her to a far-off boarding school. He knew every inch of this house and none of it had ever been his; none of it had ever been safe. He was as much a prop as any of the other things Violet surrounded herself with—only unlike the vases, he loved her despite knowing how easily and unrepentantly she'd use him.

He followed the bright hall toward Violet's quarters, knowing how much she liked to spend her days in the office there with its views of the city she'd conquered. He had memories of catapulting himself down this same hallway as a child, careening off the walls and coming to a skidding halt in that room, only to climb up on the chaise and lie at his mother's feet as she'd run her lines and practiced her voices, her various accents, the postures that made her body into someone else's. He'd found her fascinating, back then. He supposed he still did, and Giancarlo couldn't remember, then, at what age he'd realized that Violet was better admired than depended upon. That her love was a distantly beautiful thing, better experienced as a fan than a family member. The first time she'd released a photo of him he'd found embarrassing? Or the tenth, with as little remorse?

He only knew they'd both been far happier once he'd accepted it.

Giancarlo paused in the doorway, hearing his mother's famous laugh before he saw her. She wasn't in her usual place today, reclining on her chaise like the Empress of Hollywood. She was standing at the French doors instead, bathed in soft light from the summer day beyond with a mobile phone in her hand, and even though there was no denying her celebrated beauty, his gaze went straight to the other woman in the room as if Violet wasn't there at all.

Paige sat at the fussy little desk in the corner, typing something as a male voice responded to whatever Violet had said from her mobile phone, obviously on speaker. Paige was frowning down at her laptop as her fingers flew over the keys, and when Violet turned toward her to roll her eyes at her assistant, Giancarlo could see the face Paige made in immediate response.

Sympathetic. Fully on Violet's side. Staunch and true, he'd have said, if he didn't know better.

He'd seen that expression before. *That* was the woman he'd loved in all the passionate fury of those two months of madness. Stalwart. Loyal. Not in any way the kind of woman who would sell a man out and print it all up in the tabloids. He'd have sworn on that. He'd have gambled everything.

Giancarlo still couldn't believe how wrong he'd been.

His stomach twisted, and it took everything he had not to make a noise, not to bellow out his fury at all of this—but mostly at himself.

Because he wanted to believe, still. Despite everything. He wanted there to be an explanation for what had happened ten years ago. He wanted Paige—and when had he started thinking about her by that name, without stumbling over it at all?—to be who she appeared to be. Dedicated to his mother. Deeply sorry for what had gone before, and with some *reason* for what she'd done. And not the kind of self-serving reason Violet always had…

He wanted her back.

And that was when Giancarlo woke up with a jolt and recognized the danger he was in. History could not repeat itself. Not with her. Not ever.

"Darling," Violet said when she ended her call, turning from the window and smiling at him. "Don't lurk in the hallway. It was only my agent. A whinier, more demanding fool I have yet to meet, and yet I'm fairly certain he's the best there is."

But what Giancarlo noticed was the way Paige straightened in her chair, her eyes wide and blue when they flew to him, then quickly shuttered when she looked back to her keyboard.

He could think of a greater fool than his mother's parasitical agent. It was something about finding himself back in Los Angeles, he thought as he fought back his own temper, as well as seeing Paige again. It would have been different if he'd encountered her in some other city. Somewhere that held no trace of who they'd been together. But here, their history curled around everything, like a thick, encroaching smog, and made it impossible to inhale without confronting it every time.

With every goddamned breath.

"I must return to Italy," he said shortly. Almost as if he wasn't certain he'd say it at all if he didn't say it quickly and that, of course, made him despise himself all the more.

"You can't leave," Violet said at once. Giancarlo noticed Paige seemed to type even more furiously and failed to raise her head at all. "You've only just arrived."

"I came because it had been an unconscionably long time, Mother," he said softly. "It was never my intention to stay away so long. But I have a solution."

"You are moving back to Los Angeles," Violet said, a curve to her mouth that suggested she didn't believe it even as she said it. "I'm delighted. That Malibu house is far too nice to waste on all those renters."

"Not at all." He wanted to study Paige instead of his mother but he didn't dare. Still, he was as aware of her as if she was triple her own size. As if she loomed there in his peripheral vision, a great dark cloud, consuming everything. "You must come to Italy. Bring your assistant. Stay for the rest of the summer."

Violet looked startled for a moment, but then in the next her face smoothed out, and he recognized the mask she wore then. As impenetrable as it was graceful. A vision of loveliness that showed only what she wanted seen, and nothing else. Violet Sutherlin, the star. Giancarlo didn't know what it said about him that he found this version of her easier to handle than the one who pretended motherhood was her primary concern.

"Darling, you know my feelings about Italy," she murmured, and a stranger might have believed her wry, easy tone. "I love it with all my heart. But I'm afraid I buried that heart with your father."

"Not that Italy," he said. He smiled, though he understood he was speaking as much to the silent woman in the corner of his eye as to his mother. "My Italy."

"Do you have your own?" Violet asked. She laughed again. "You have been busy indeed."

"I've completely transformed the estate," Giancarlo said quietly. "I know we've discussed all these changes over the years, but I'd like you to see them for yourself. I think Father would be proud."

"I know he would," Violet said with a glimmer of something raw in her gaze and the sound of it in her voice, and Giancarlo knew he had her. Paige knew it too, he could tell. He felt more than saw her stiffen at her desk, and it took everything he had to keep the triumph from his voice, the sheer victory from his face. "Of course, Giancarlo. I'd love to see Tuscany again."

He only let himself look at Paige again when he was certain he had himself under complete control. *Like iron,* he thought fiercely. Like the old houses he'd rebuilt on the ancestral estate in Tuscany, stone by ancient stone, forcing his will and vision onto every acre.

He would take her away from Los Angeles, where history seemed to infuse every moment between them with meaning he didn't want. He didn't know why he hadn't thought of this sooner.

In the far reaches of Tuscany, as remote as it was possible to get in one of the most famous and beloved regions of the world, she would be entirely dependent on him. Violet could relax in the hands of his world-class staff, her every need anticipated and met, and he would have all the time in the world to vanquish this demon from his past, for good. All the time he needed to truly make her pay.

Because that was what he wanted, he reminded himself. To make her pay. Everything else was memory and fantasy and better suited to a long night's dream than reality.

"Wonderful." Giancarlo tried not to gloat, and knew he failed when Paige frowned. And it was still a victory. It was still a plan. And it would work, he was sure of it. Because it had to. "We leave tonight."

Paige had dreamed of Italy her whole life.

When she was a child, she'd sneaked library books into her mother's bleak trailer in the blistering heat of the rocky Arizona desert. She'd waited for Arleen to pass out before she'd lost herself in them, and she'd dreamed. Fierce dreams of cypress trees in stern columns marching across a deep green undulation of ancient fields. Monuments to long lost gods and civilizations gone centuries before her birth, red-roofed towns clustered on gentle hills beneath a soft, Italian sun.

Then she'd met Giancarlo, who carried the lilt of Italy in every word he spoke, and her dreams had taken on a more specific shape. Even back then, when he'd wanted to play around in Hollywood more than he'd wanted to tend to his heritage, he'd spoken of the thousands of rural acres that his father had only just started to reclaim from the encroaching wilderness of a generation or two of neglect. They were his birthright and in those giddy days ten years ago she'd dared to imagine that she was, too.

And now she was finally here, and it turned out it was extraordinarily painful to visit a place that she'd once imagined might be her home and now knew never, ever would be. More than painful—but she told herself it was the jet lag that made her ache like that. Nothing a good night's sleep on solid ground wouldn't cure.

Even if it was *this* solid ground.

The vast estate sprawled across a part of Tuscany that had been in the Alessi family in one form or another since the Middle Ages. It was dotted with old farmhouses Giancarlo had spent the past decade painstakingly renovating for a very special class of clientele: people as wealthy as his mother and as allergic to invasions of their privacy as his father had been. As Paige supposed he must be himself now, after his too-public shaming at her own hands.

Here at Castello Alessi and all across its hilly lands, thick with olive groves and vineyards, lavender bushes and timeless forests of oak trees—according to the splashy website Paige had accessed a hundred times before and once again from the plane when she'd accepted she was really, truly coming here at last—such privacy-minded people could relax, secure in the knowledge that the "cottages" they'd paid dearly either to rent or to buy outright and fashion to their liking were as private and remote as it was possible to get while still enjoying world-class service akin to that of the finest hotels, thanks to Giancarlo's private, around-the-clock staff.

But none of that applied to Paige, she was well aware.

They'd landed on a private airstrip in a nearby valley after flying all night. It had been a bright, somehow distinctly Italian summer morning, filled with yellow flowers and too-blue skies, and a waiting driver had whisked them off to the estate some forty minutes away. It was a long, gorgeous drive, winding in and around the hills of Tuscany that looked exactly as Paige had imagined them while also being somehow so much *more* than she'd anticipated. Violet had been installed in the lavishly remodeled *castello* itself, arrayed around a welcoming stone courtyard with heart-stopping views and her own private spa with waiting staff to pamper her at once, as if she was truly the High Queen of Italy.

Paige, on the other hand, Giancarlo ushered into a Jeep and then personally drove far out into the heart of the property, until all she could see in all directions was the gently rolling countryside and one lone house at the top of the nearest hill. All of it so gorgeous and yet so *familiar*, as if she'd been here before and recognized it like a homecoming, and yet, she was forced to keep telling herself, none of this was hers. Not the perfect sky, the charming lane, the pretty little houses on this or that ridge. *Not hers.* The man beside her least of all.

"Are you deliberately stranding me out here as some kind of punishment?" she asked him, when it became clear that a smaller cottage down in the valley beneath that lone house was where he was headed. She was doing her best not to look at him, braced beside her in the smaller-by-the-moment front of his Jeep as they bumped along the lazy dirt road that meandered toward the little stone house, because she was afraid it might make all these raw emotions inside of her spill over into tears. Or worse. "Don't you think that looks a little bit strange?"

"My mother will be waited on hand and foot in the *castello*," he said, his gruff voice either impatient or triumphant, and Paige couldn't tell which. She wasn't sure she wanted to know. "And if by some chance she needs you while undergoing a battalion of spa treatments, never fear, the Wi-Fi is excellent. I trust she can manage to send out an email should she require your presence."

"So the answer is yes," Paige said stiffly as he pulled up in front of the cottage. He turned the key in the ignition and the sudden quiet seemed to pour in through the open windows, as terrifying as it was sweet. "This is a punishment."

"Yes," he said in that low way of his that wrapped around her and made her yearn, then made her question her own sanity. "I am punishing you with Tuscany. It is a fate worse than death, obviously. Just look around."

She didn't want to look around, for a thousand complicated reasons and none she'd dare admit. It made her feel scraped to the bone and weak. So very weak. So she looked at him instead, which wasn't really any better.

"You think I don't know why you brought me here, but of course I do." She laughed, though it was a hollow little sound and seemed to make that scraped sensation expand inside of her. "You're making sure I have nowhere to run. I think that counts as the most basic of torture methods, doesn't it?"

"Correction." He aimed a smile at her that didn't quite

reach the storm in his eyes, but made her feel edgy all the same. "I don't care if you know. It isn't the same thing."

Paige pushed her way out of the Jeep, not surprised when he climbed out himself. Was this all a prologue to another one of these scenes with him—as damaging as it was irresistible? She tucked her hands into the pockets of the jeans she'd worn on the long flight and wished she felt like herself. *It's only jet lag,* she assured herself. Or so she hoped. *You've read about jet lag. Everyone says it passes or no one would ever go anywhere, would they?* But she didn't feel particularly tired. She felt stripped to the bone instead. Flayed wide-open.

And the way he looked at her didn't help.

"How long?" she asked, her voice not quite sounding like her own. "How long do you think you can keep me here?"

Giancarlo pulled her bags from the back and carried them to the door of the cottage, shouldering it open and disappearing inside. But Paige stayed where she was, next to the Jeep with her eyes on the rolling green horizon. The sweet blue of the summer sky was packed with fluffy white clouds that looked as if they were made of meringue and were far more beautiful than all of her dreams put together, and she tried her best not to cry, because this was a prison—she knew it was—and yet she couldn't escape the notion that it was *home*.

"I'll keep you as long as I like," he said from the doorway, his voice another rolling thing through the morning's stillness, like a dark shadow beneath all that shine. "This is about my satisfaction, *cara.* Not your feelings. Or it wouldn't be torture, would it? It would be a holiday."

"By your account, I imagine I don't have any feelings anyway, isn't that right?" She hadn't meant to say that, and certainly not in that challenging tone. She scowled at the stunning view, and reminded herself that she'd never really had a home and never would. Longing for a place like this was nothing more than masochistic, no matter how familiar it felt. "I'm nothing but a mercenary bitch who set out to destroy you once and is now, what? A delusional stalker who has insinuated herself into the middle of your family? For my own nefarious purposes, none of which have been in evidence at all over the past three years?"

"I find *parasite* covers all the bases." Giancarlo drawled that out, and it was worse, somehow, here in the midst of so much prettiness. Like a creeping black thing in the center of all that green, worse than a mere shadow. "No need to succumb to theatrics when you can merely call it what it is."

She shook her head, that same old anguish moving inside of her, making her shake deep in her gut, making her wish for things she knew better than to want. A home, at last. Love to fill it. A place to belong and a person to share it with—

Paige had always *known better*. Dreams were one thing. They were harmless. No one could have survived the hard, barren place where she'd grown up, first her embittered mother's teenage mistake and then her meal ticket, without a few dreams to keep them going. Much less what had happened ten years ago. What her mother had become. What Paige had nearly had to do in a vain attempt to save her.

But *wishes* were nothing but borrowed trouble. And she supposed, looking back, that had been the issue from the start—being with Giancarlo had made her imagine she could dare to want things she knew, *she knew,* could never be hers. Never.

You won't make that mistake again in a hurry, her mother's caustic voice jeered at her.

Paige risked a look at Giancarlo then, despairing at the way her heart squeezed tight at the sight of him the way it always had, at that dark look on his face that was half hunger and half dislike, at the way she had always loved him and understood she always would, and to what end? He would have his revenge and she would endure it and somehow, somehow, she would survive him, too.

It hurts a little bit more today than it usually does because you're here and you're tired, she tried to tell herself. *But you're fine. You're always fine. Or you will be.*

"I know you don't want to believe me," she said, because she had always been such an idiot where this man was concerned. She had never had the slightest idea how to protect herself. Giancarlo had been the kind of man who had blistering affairs the way other people had dinner plans, but *she* had fallen head over heels in love with him at first glance and destroyed them both in the process. And now she wanted, so desperately, for him to *see* her, just for a moment. The real her. "But I would do anything for your mother. For a hundred different reasons. Chief among them that she's been better to me than my own mother ever was."

"And here I thought you emerged fully grown from a bed of lies," he said silkily. He paused, his dark eyes on her, as if recognizing how rare it was that Paige mentioned her own mother—but she watched him shrug it off instead of pursuing it and told herself it was for the best. "I was avoiding the city my mother lived in all these years and the kind of people who lived in it, not my mother. A crucial distinction, because believe me, *Paige*, I would also do anything for my mother. And I will."

There was a threat in the last three words. A promise. And there was no particular reason it should thud into her so hard, as if it might have taken her from her feet if she hadn't already been braced against all of this. The pretty place, the sense of homecoming, the knowledge he was even more lost to her when he stood in front of her than he had been in all their years apart.

"I loved my mother, too, Giancarlo," Paige said, and she understood it was that scraped raw feeling that made her say such a thing. Giancarlo would never understand the kind of broken, terrible excuse for love that was the only kind Paige had ever known, before him. The sharp, scarring toll it exacted. How it festered inside and taught a person how to see the world only through the lens of it, no matter how blurred or cracked or deeply twisted. "And that never got me anything but bruises and a broken heart." And then had taken the only things that had ever mattered to her. She swallowed. "I know the difference."

He moved out of the doorway of the cottage then, closing the distance between them with a few sure steps, and Paige couldn't tell if that was worse or better. Everything seemed too mixed up and impossible and somehow *right*, too; the gentle green trees and the soft, lavender-scented breeze, and his dark gold eyes in the center of the world, making her heart beat loud and slow inside her chest.

Stop it, she ordered herself. *This is not your home. Neither is he.*

"Is this an appeal to my better nature?" Giancarlo asked softly. Dangerously. "I keep telling you, that man is dead. Killed by your own hand. Surely you must realize this by now."

"I know." She tilted up her chin and hoped he couldn't see how lost she felt. How utterly out of place. How hideously dislocated if it seemed that *he* was the only steady thing here, this man who detested her. "And here I am. Isolated and at your beck and call. Just think of all the ways you can make me pay for your untimely death."

She couldn't read the shadow that moved over his face then. His hand moved as if it was outside his control and he ran the backs of his fingers over the line of her jaw, softly, so softly, and yet she knew better than to mistake his gentleness for kindness. She knew better than to trust her body's interpretations of things when it came to this man and the things he could do to it with so seemingly careless a touch.

The truth was in that fierce look in his eyes, that flat line of his delectable mouth. The painful truth that nothing she said could change, or would.

He wanted to hurt her. He wanted all of this to *hurt*.

"Believe me," he said quietly. Thickly, as if that scraped raw thing was in him, too. "I have thought of little else."

Paige thought he might kiss her then, and that masochist in her *yearned* for it, no matter what came after. No matter how he made her pay for wanting him, which she knew he would. She swayed forward and lifted her mouth toward his and for a moment his attention seemed to drift toward her lips—

But then he muttered one of those curses that sounded almost pretty because it was in Italian. And he stepped back, staring at her as if she was a ghost. A demon, more like. Sent to destroy him when it was clear to her that if there was going to be any destruction here, it would be at his hands.

It was going to be her in pieces, not him. And Paige didn't understand why she didn't care about that the way she should. When he looked at her, she didn't care about anything but him and all these terrible, pointless wishes that had wrecked her once already. She should have learned her lesson a long time ago. She'd thought she had.

"I suggest you rest," he said in a clipped tone, stalking back toward the driver's side of the Jeep. "Dinner will be served at sunset and you'll wake up starving sometime before then. That's always the way with international flights."

As if he knew she'd never left the country before, when she'd thought she'd hidden it well today. His knowing anyway seemed too intimate, somehow. The sort of detail a lover might know, or perhaps a friend, and he was neither. She told herself she was being ridiculous, but it was hard to keep looking at him when she felt there had to be far too much written across her face then. Too much of that Arizona white trash dust, showing him all the things about her she'd gone to such lengths to keep him from ever knowing.

"At the *castello*?" she asked, after the moment stretched on too long and his expression had begun to edge into impatience as he stood there, the Jeep in between them and his hand on the driver's door. "That seems like a bit of a walk. It was a twenty-minute drive, at least."

"At the house on the hill," he said, and jerked his head toward the farmhouse that squatted at the top of the nearest swell of pretty green, looking sturdy and complacent in the sunlight, all light stones and an impressive loggia. "Right there. Unless that's too much of a hike for you these days, now that you live on a Bel Air estate and are neck deep in opulence day and night. None of it earned. Or yours."

Paige ignored the slap. "That really all depends on who lives there," she replied, and it was remarkably hard to make her voice sound anything approximating *light*.

"A troll? The Italian bogeyman? The big, bad wolf with his terrible fangs?"

His mouth moved into that crooked thing that made her stomach flip over and her heart ache. More. Again. *Always.*

"That would be me," he said softly, and she thought he took a certain pleasure in it. "So that's all of the above, I'd think. For your sins."

A long nap and a very hot shower after she woke made Paige feel like a new person. Or herself again, at last. She had been too weary and inexplicably sad to explore the cottage when Giancarlo had driven away, so she did it now, with the whisper-soft robe she'd found in the master bathroom wrapped around her and her feet bare against the reclaimed stone floors, her wet hair feeling indulgent against her shoulders as she moved through the charming space.

It was a two-story affair in what had looked from the outside like a very old stone outbuilding. Inside, it was filled with the early-evening light thanks to the tall windows everywhere, the exposed beams high above, and the fact the interior was wholly open to best take advantage of what would otherwise have felt like a small space. Stairs led from the stone ground floor to the loft above, which featured a large, extraordinarily comfortable bed in the airy room nestled in the eaves, a small sitting area with a balcony beyond, and the luxurious master bath Paige had just enjoyed.

The main floor was divided into an efficient, cheerful kitchen with a happily stocked refrigerator, a cozy sitting area with deep sofas arranged around a wide stone fireplace, a small dining area that led out to a patio that spanned the length of the cottage and led into a small, well-tended garden. And everywhere she looked, behind everything and hovering near and far and more beautiful by the moment, the Tuscan view.

Home, she thought, despite herself.

Evening had crept in with long, deep shadows that settled in the valley and made art out of the soft green trees, the cypress sentries and the rounded hills on all sides. The road that had felt torturously remote when Giancarlo had driven her here looked like something from one of her beloved old books now, winding off into the distance or off into dreams. Paige stood there in the window until the air cooled around her, and realized only when she started back up the stairs that she hadn't breathed like that—deeply and fully, all the way down to her feet, the way she had when she'd danced—in a very long time.

Almost as if she was comfortable here. As if she belonged. She'd felt that way in only one other place in her whole life, and had been as wrong. Giancarlo's Malibu home, all wood and glass, angled to best let the sea in, had only been a pretty house. This was a pretty place.

And when you leave here, she told herself harshly, *you will never come back. The same as that house in Malibu. Everyone feels at home in affluent places. That's what they're built to do.*

Paige dressed slowly and carefully, her nerves prickling into a new awareness as she rifled through her suitcase. Should she wear the sort of thing she would wear if this was a vacation in Italy she happened to be taking by herself? Or should she wear something she suspected Giancarlo would prefer, so he could better enact his revenge? On the one hand, jeans and a slouchy sweatshirt, all comfort and very little style. On the other, a flirty little dress he could *get his hands under,* like before. She didn't have the slightest idea which way to go.

"What do *you* want?" she asked her sleepy-eyed reflection in the bathroom mirror, her voice throaty from all that sleep.

But that was the trouble. She still wanted the same things she'd always wanted. She could admit that, here and now, with Giancarlo's Italy pressing in on her from all sides. The difference was that this time, she knew better than to imagine she'd get it.

Paige dried her hair slowly, her mind oddly empty even as the rest of her felt tight with all the things she didn't want to think about directly. Taut and on edge. She pulled on a pair of soft white trousers and a loose sort of tunic on top, a compromise between the jeans she'd have preferred and what she assumed Giancarlo would likely want to see her wear, given the circumstances.

"What he'd really like is me, as naked as the day I was born and crawling up that hillside on my hands and knees," she muttered out loud and then laughed at the image, the sound creaky and strange in the quiet of the cottage. She kept laughing until a wet heat pricked at the back of her eyes and she had to pull in a ragged breath to keep the tears from pouring over. Then another.

Paige frowned as she slipped her feet into a pair of thonged flat sandals. When was the last time she'd laughed like that? About anything?

What a sad creature you've become, she scolded herself as she dug out her smartphone from her bag and scrolled through her messages. But the truth was, she had always been a fairly sad thing, when she looked back at the progression of her life. Sad and studious or determined and stubborn, from the start. It had been the only way to survive the chaos that had been her mother. There had only been one two-month stretch of laughter in her life, gleaming and overflowing and dizzy with joy, and she'd ruined it ten years ago.

"My goodness," Violet said in her grand way when she picked up her private line, after Paige apologized for disappearing and then sleeping for hours, "this is *Italia,* Paige. One must soak in *la dolce vita,* especially when jet-lagged. I plan to spend the night in my lovely little castle, getting fat on all the *marvelous* local cuisine! I suggest you do the same."

And Paige would have loved to do the same, she thought when she finally stepped out of her cottage into the cool evening, the Tuscan sky turning to gold above her. But she had a date with her sins instead.

Sins that felt like wishes granted, and what was wrong with her that she didn't want to tell the difference between the two?

She took her time and yet the walk was still too short. Much too short.

And Giancarlo waited there at the crest of the hill, his eyes as hard as his body appeared loose and relaxed, in linen trousers and the sort of camel-colored sport coat that made her think of his aristocratic roots and her lack of them. And Paige was suddenly as wide-awake as if she'd drowned herself in a vat of espresso.

He looked like something more than a man as he waited there, at first a shadow next to the bold upright thrust of a thick cypress tree, then, as she drew closer, very distinctly himself. He'd clearly watched her come all the way up the side of his hill, and she wasn't sure if she'd seen him from afar without realizing it or if it was that odd magnetic pull inside of her that had done it, pointing her toward him as unerringly as if she'd been headed straight to him all along.

Home, that thing in her whispered, and she didn't have

the strength to pretend she didn't feel it when she did. Not tonight.

She stopped when she was still some distance away and looked back the way she'd come, unable to keep the small sigh of pleasure from escaping her lips. There was the hint of mist in the valley the lower the sun inched toward the hills, adding an elegant sort of haunting to the shadows that danced between them, and far off in the distance the *castello* stood tall and proud, lights blazing against the coming night. It was so quiet and perfect and deeply satisfying in a way Paige hadn't known anything could be. Gooseflesh prickled up and down her arms and she felt it all like a heavy sob in her chest, rolling through her, threatening her very foundations.

Or maybe that was him. Maybe it had always been him.

"It's gorgeous here," she said, which felt deeply inadequate. "It doesn't seem real."

"My father believed that the land is our bones," Giancarlo said. "Protect it, and we strengthen ourselves. Conserve it and care for it, and we become greater in its glory. Sometimes I think he was a madman, a farmer hiding in an aristocrat's body." His gaze moved over her face, then beyond her, toward the setting sun. "And then another sunset reminds me that he was right. Beauty is always worth it. It feeds the soul."

"He sounds like some kind of poet."

"Not my father. Poets and artists were to be championed, as one must always support art and culture for the same reason one tends the land, but Alessis had a higher calling." He shook his head. "Endless debt and responsibility, apparently. I might have been better off as an artist, come to that."

"If I had a home like this, I don't think I'd mind doing

whatever it took to keep it," Paige said then. She remembered herself. "I don't think anyone would."

She thought Giancarlo smiled, though his face was obscured in the falling dark and then she knew she must have imagined it, because this wasn't that kind of evening no matter how lovely it was. He wasn't that kind of man. Not anymore. Not for her.

"Come," he said. He reached out his hand and held it there in the last gasp of golden light, and Paige knew, somehow, that everything would be divided into before and after she took it. The world. Her life. This *thing* that was still between them. And that precarious, wildly beating creature inside her chest that was the battered ruins of her heart.

His mouth crooked slightly as the moment stretched out. She made no move; she was frozen into place and wasn't sure she could do anything about it, but he didn't drop his hand.

"Did you make me dinner?" she asked, her voice shockingly light when there was nothing but heaviness and their history and her treacherous heart inside of her, and she thought neither one of them was fooled. "Because food poisoning really would be a punishment, all joking aside."

"I am Italian," he said, with a note of amused outrage in his voice, which reminded her too strongly of all that laughter they'd shared a lifetime ago. As if the only things that had mattered in the whole world had been there in his smile. She'd thought so then. She thought maybe she still did, for all the good that would do her here. "Of course I can cook." He paused, as if noticing how friendly he sounded and remembering how inappropriate that was tonight. As if he, too, was finding it hard to recall the battle lines he'd drawn. "But even if I couldn't, the estate has a fleet of chefs on call. Meals are always gourmet here, no matter who prepares them."

"Careful," she said softly, more to her memories and her silly heart than the man who stood there before her, still reaching out to her, still her greatest temptation made flesh. Still the perfect embodiment of all the things she'd always wanted and couldn't have. "I might forget to be suitably intimidated and start enjoying myself. And then what would happen?"

He definitely smiled that time, and Paige felt it like a deep, golden fire, lighting her up from the inside out. Making her shiver.

"Surrender takes many forms," he replied into the indigo twilight that cloaked them both, now that the sun had finally sunk beneath the furthest hill. "I want yours every way I can get it."

"I can surrender to *la dolce vita*," she said, as airily as possible, as if her tone of voice might make it so. "I understand that's the point of Italy."

He still stood there, his hand out, as if he could stand like that forever. "That's as good a place to start as any."

And there was no real decision, in the end. There had been so many choices along the way, hadn't there? Paige could have got a different job three years ago. She could have left Violet's house and employ the moment Giancarlo had appeared, or anytime since. She could have declined the offer of that "date" that night, she could have stayed standing up instead of sinking to her knees by the side of that road, she could have shown him nothing in Violet's closet that day but her back as she walked away from him. She could have refused to board his plane, refused to leave her cottage tonight, locked herself inside rather than climb this hill to stand before him like this.

He hadn't *happened* to her, like the weather. She'd

chosen this, every step of the way, and even here, even stranded in the countryside with this man who thought so ill of her, she felt more at home than she had in years. Maybe ever. She supposed that meant she'd made her decision a long time ago.

So Paige reached out her hand and slid it into his. She let the heat of him wash through her at that faintly rough touch, his palm warm and strong and perfect, and told herself it didn't matter what happened next.

That she'd surrendered herself to Giancarlo a long time ago, whether he understood that or not.

CHAPTER FIVE

"IF THIS IS your revenge," Paige said, a current of laughter in her voice though her expression was mild, "I think I should confess to you that it tastes a whole lot like red wine."

He should do something about that, Giancarlo thought, watching her move through the refurbished ground floor of his renovated house. She was still so graceful, so light on her feet. Like poetry in motion, and he'd never been able to reconcile how she could flow like that and have turned out so rotten within. He'd never understood it.

It doesn't matter what you understand, he snapped at himself. *Only what you do to make this* thing *for her go away—*

But something had happened out there as the sun set. Something had shifted inside him, though he couldn't quite identify it. He wasn't certain he'd want to name it if he could.

"It may prove to be a long night, *cara*," he told her darkly, pouring himself a glass of the wine they made here from Alessi grapes. "This is merely the beginning."

"The civilized version of revenge, then," she murmured, almost as if to herself, running her fingers along the length of the reclaimed wood table that marked his dining area in the great, open space he'd done himself.

In soothing yet bright colors and historically contextual pieces, all of which dimmed next to that effortless, off-handed beauty of hers. "I'll keep that in mind."

This didn't feel like revenge. This felt like a memory. Giancarlo didn't want to think too closely about that, but the truth of it slapped at him all the same. It could have been any one of the long, lush evenings they'd shared in Malibu a decade back that still shimmered in his recollection, as if the two of them had been lit from within. It shimmered in him now, too. Again. As if this was the culmination of all the dreams he'd lied and told himself he'd never had, in all those years since he'd left Los Angeles and started bringing the estate back to life.

There was too much history between them, too much that had gone wrong to ever fix, and yet he still caught himself watching her as if this was a new beginning. But then, he had always been such a damned fool where this woman was concerned, hadn't he?

Earlier he'd stood in the courtyard of the *castello* with Violet, toasting her first night back in Italy since his father's funeral eight years ago, and he'd felt a sense of deep rightness. Of homecoming, long overdue. These hills held his happiest childhood memories, after all. When his parents had both been alive, and in those early years, so much in love it had colored the air around them.

"You've done a marvelous thing here, darling," Violet had said, smiling as much at him as at the achingly perfect view.

"I remember the days when we couldn't drive out the gates in Bel Air without having to fight our way through packs of photographers," he'd said, gazing out at the slumbering hills, all of them his now, his birthright and his future. His responsibility. And not a single paparazzo in a thousand miles or more. No lies. No stories. Only the enduring beauty of the earth. "Just to get to school in the morning."

"The tabloids giveth and the tabloids taketh away," Violet had said drily, looking as chic and elegant as ever though she wore her version of lounge wear and what was, for her, a practically cosmetic-free face. "It's never been particularly easy to navigate, I grant you, but there did used to be a line. Or perhaps I'm kidding myself."

"I want this place to be a refuge," he'd told her then. "It's nearly fifteen miles to the nearest main road. Everything is private. It's the perfect retreat for people who can't hide anywhere else."

Violet had tasted her wine and she'd taken her time looking at him again, and he'd still been unsure if she was pausing for dramatic effect or if that was simply how she processed emotion. She was still a mystery to him and he'd long since accepted she always would be. Or anyway, he'd been telling himself he'd accepted it. It might even have been true.

"Yes," she'd said, "and it's very beautiful. It's always been beautiful. I imagine I could live here quite happily and transform myself into one of those portly, Italy-maddened expatriates who are forever writing those merry little Tuscan memoirs and waxing rhapsodic about the *light*." Her brows had lifted. "But which one of us is it that feels they need a hiding place, Giancarlo? Is that meant to be you or me?"

"Never fear, Mother," he'd replied evenly. "I have no intention of having children of my own. I won't have any cause to hide away, the better to protect them from prying eyes and a judgmental world. Perhaps I, too, will flourish in the heat of so many spotlights."

She'd only smiled, enigmatic as ever, seemingly not in the least bit chastised by what he'd said. Had he expected otherwise? "Privacy can be overrated, my darling boy. Particularly when it better resembles a jail."

And now he stood in the cheerful lounge of the house he'd taken apart and put back together with his own two hands, and watched the woman he'd once loved more than any other walk through the monument—he wouldn't call it a *jail*—he'd built to his own unhappiness, his lonely, broken, betrayed heart.

How had he failed to realize, until this moment, that he'd built it for her? That he'd been hiding here these past ten years—deliberately keeping himself some kind of hermit, tucked away on this property and in this very cottage? That it was as much his refuge *for* her as it was *from* her?

That notion made something like a storm howl in him, deep and long. And as if she could read his mind, Paige turned, a small smile on that distracting mouth of hers.

"I always liked your films," she said, her voice the perfect complement to the carefully decorated great room, the furnishings a mix of masculine ease and his Italian heritage, as if he'd planned for her to stand there in its center and make it all work. "I suppose it shouldn't surprise me that that kind of attention to detail should spill over into all the things you do."

"My films were laughable vanity projects at best," he told her, that storm in his voice and clawing at the walls of his chest. "I should never have taken myself seriously, much less allowed anyone else to do the same. It's an embarrassment."

Paige wrinkled her nose and he thought that might kill him, because finding her *adorable* was far more dangerous than simply wanting her. One was about sex, which was simple. The other had consequences. Terrible consequences he refused to pay.

"I liked them."

"Shall we talk about the things you like?" Giancarlo asked, and he sounded overbearingly brooding to his own ears. As if he was performing a role because he thought the moment needed a villain, not because he truly wanted to put her back in her place. "Your interest in photography and amateur porn, for instance?"

Some revenge, he thought darkly. *Next you'll try to cuddle her to death with your words.*

But she only smiled in that enigmatic way of hers, and moved closer to one of the paintings on the wall, her hands cupped around her glass of wine and that inky black hair of hers falling in abandon down her back, and it wasn't cuddling he thought about as he watched her move. Then bite her lower lip as she peered up at the painting. It wasn't *cuddling* that made his blood heat and his mouth dry.

"I don't understand why I'm here," Paige said, so softly that it took him a moment to realize she'd spoken. She swiveled back to look at him, framed there like a snapshot, the woman who had destroyed him before the great, bright canvas that stretched high behind her, all shapes and emotion and a swirl of color, that he hadn't understood until tonight had reminded him of her.

Giancarlo told himself it was a sour realization, but his sex felt heavy and the air between them tasted thick. Like desire. Like need.

Like fate.

"It seems as if you've achieved what you set out to do," she continued as if she couldn't feel the thickness, though he knew, somehow, that she could. "You've separated me from Violet without seeming to do so deliberately, which I'm assuming was your purpose from the start. But why bring me all the way here? Why not leave me in California and spirit Violet away? And having made me come all the way here," Paige continued, something he couldn't identify making her eyes gleam green in the mellow light, "why not simply leave me to rot in my little cottage? It's pretty as prison cells go, I grant you. Very pretty. It might take me weeks to realize I'm well and truly trapped there."

He let his gaze roam over her the way his hands itched to do. "You've forgotten the most important part."

"The sex, yes," Paige supplied, and she didn't sound particularly cowed by the idea, or even as outraged as she'd been back in Los Angeles. Her tone was bland. Perhaps too bland. "On command."

"I was going to say obedience," he said, and he didn't feel as if he was playing a game any longer. He was too busy letting his eyes trace over her curves, letting his hands relish the tactile memory of her face between them as if she'd burned her way into his flesh. He could still taste her, damn it. And he wanted more.

"Obedience," she repeated, as if testing each syllable of the word as she said it. "Does that include feeding me a gourmet dinner in this perfect little mansion only a *count* would call a cottage? Are you entirely sure you know what *obedience* involves?"

Giancarlo smiled, or anyway, his mouth moved. "That's the point. It involves whatever I say it involves."

He took a sip of his wine as he walked over to the open glass doors that led out to the loggia, nodding for her to join him outside. Stiffly, carefully—as if she was more shaken by their encounter than she appeared, and God help him, he wanted that to be true—she did.

Because the truth was so pathetic, wasn't it? He still so badly wanted her to be real. To have meant some part of the things that had happened between them. All these years later, he still wanted that. Giancarlo despaired of himself.

A table waited out in the soft night air, bright with candles and laden with local produce and delicacies prepared on-site, while a rolling cart sat next to it with even more tempting dishes beneath silver covers. It was achingly romantic, precisely as he'd ordered. The hills and valleys of the estate rolled out beneath the stars, with lights winking here and there in the distance, making their isolation high up on this terrace at a remove from all the world seem profound.

That, too, was the point.

He moved to pull her chair out for her like the parody of the perfect gentleman he had never quite been and waited as she settled in, taking a moment to inhale her scent. Tonight she smelled of the high-end bath products he had his staff stock in the cottages, vanilla and apricots, and that hint of pure woman beneath.

"This house was a ruin when I started working on it," he told her, still standing behind her, because he didn't know what his face might show and he didn't want her to see it. To see *him*. He succumbed to a whim and ran his fingers through her hair, reveling in the heavy weight of the dark strands even as he remembered all the other times she'd wrapped him in the heat and sweetness of it. When she'd crawled over him in that wide bed in Malibu and let her hair slip and tumble all over his skin as she tortured him with that sweet mouth of hers, driving them both wild. Giancarlo hardened, remembering it, and her hair was thick silk in his hands. "It sits on its original foundation, but everything else is changed. Perhaps the walls still stand, but everything inside is new, reclaimed, or altered entirely. It might look the same from a distance, but it isn't."

"I appreciate the metaphor," Paige said, with a certain grittiness to her voice that he suspected meant her teeth were clenched. He smiled.

"Then I hope you'll appreciate this, too," he said as he rounded the table and sat down across from her, stretching out his legs before him as he did. "This is the Italian countryside and everything you can see in every direction is mine. You could scream for days and no one would hear you. You could try to escape and, unless you've taken up marathon running in your spare time, you'd run out of energy long before you found the road. You claimed to be obedient in Los Angeles because it suited you. You wanted your job more than you minded the loss of your self-respect, such as it is. Here?" He shrugged as he topped up their wineglasses with a bottle crafted from grapes he'd grown himself and then sat back, watching her closely, as she visibly fought not to react to his cool tone, his calmly belligerent words. "You have no other choice."

"That's not at all creepy," Paige said, though he could have sworn that gleam of green in her chameleon gaze was amusement, however beleaguered. "I'm definitely the terrifying stalker in this scenario, not you."

Giancarlo laughed. "Not that I would care if it really was creepy, but I don't think you really think so, do you? Shall we put it to the test?"

He wanted her to push him, he understood. He wanted to see for himself. He wanted to peel those crisp white trousers from her slim hips and lick his way into her wetness and heat and know it was all for him, the way he'd once believed it was. The way he'd once believed *she* was.

Soon, he assured himself as his body reacted to that image with predictable enthusiasm. *Soon enough.*

"Again," Paige said tightly, taking a healthy gulp of

her wine, "it seems to me that there are more effective forms of payback than a romantic dinner for two, served beneath the starry night sky on what might be the most intimate terrace on the entire planet." She looked out at the view as the heavens sparkled back at her, as if they were performing for her pleasure. "I suspect you might be doing it wrong."

"Ah, Paige," Giancarlo said softly. "You lack imagination." Her eyes swung back to his and he smiled again, wider, pleased when that seemed to alarm her. "The romantic setting will only make it more poignant, will it not, when I order you to strip and sit there naked as we eat. Or when I demand that you please me with your mouth while I soak in the view. Or when I bend you over the serving table and make you scream out my name until I'm done." He let his smile deepen as her eyes went very green, and very round. "The more civilized the setting, the more debauched the act," he said mildly. "I find there is very little more effective."

She looked stunned, and then something like wistful, and he almost broke and hauled her into his arms—but somehow, *somehow*, he reined himself in. *Just a little bit longer,* he promised himself. She blinked, then coughed, and then she folded her hands together in her lap with such precision that Giancarlo knew she was torturing *herself* with all those images he'd put in her head.

Va bene.

"You say that as if this isn't the first time you've done this." Her voice was his own little victory, so raspy was it then, with that stunned heat in her gaze and that band of color high on her cheeks. "Do you spend a lot of time enacting complicated revenge fantasies, Giancarlo? Is that another one of your heretofore hidden talents—like architecture and interior design, apparently?"

"I went to architecture school after university," he said, and something about the fact she didn't know that bothered him. Had he never told her his own story? Had he been as guilty of wearing a false persona ten years ago as she had been? Had it simply been the rush, the need that had kept them in bed and focused on other things? Had it been by her design—or had it been his own selfishness at play? He shoved that disconcerting thought aside. "But when I was finished, I decided I wanted to leverage my position as Violet's son, instead. That didn't work out very well for either one of us, did it?" He reached over and removed the silver cover from the plate of antipasti in front of her, then from his own, and smiled at her when she looked confused. "The *salsicce di cinghiale* is particularly good," he told her. "And you should be certain to eat well. We have a very long night ahead of us."

He expected her to do as she was told. It took a moment or two for him to realize that she hadn't moved. That she appeared to have frozen solid where she sat and was staring at him with a stricken sort of expression on her face.

Giancarlo lifted a brow. "Was I unclear?"

"I appreciate all the tension and drama," Paige said after a moment. "I don't think I realized how very much you take after your mother until now. That's a compliment," she added in a hurry when he frowned at her. "But I'll pass."

"That is not an option you have." He shrugged. "You persist in thinking what you want comes into play here. It doesn't."

"What will you do?" she asked softly, so softly it took a moment for him to hear the challenge beneath the words, and then to see it there in her chameleon eyes.

"Make me scream for people who won't hear me? Make me walk for days in search of a road that's still hours from anywhere? Force me to stay in that gorgeous little cottage down the hill like a bird in a cage?"

"Or, alternatively, merely call my mother and tell her exactly who you are," he suggested. "A fate you felt was worse than death and far more terrible than anything I might do a week ago."

But tonight she only shook her head and she didn't avert her gaze, reminding him of that moment in his mother's closet across the world. Reminding him he'd never controlled this woman, not even when she'd agreed to let him.

"I think if you were going to do that, Giancarlo, you would have. You wouldn't have dragged me across the planet and then presented me with wine and a four-course meal."

He laughed, a smoky little sound against the night. It did nothing to ease the mounting tension. "Do you really want to test that theory?"

She leaned forward, holding his gaze, and his laughter dried up as if it had never been. He was aware of everything at once. The stars above them, the faint breeze that teased him with the intoxicating scent of her. The rich food before them, the dancing candlelight. The way she sat now, the wide neck of her brightly patterned tunic falling open as she leaned toward him, hinting at the soft curves beneath.

And all that fire, as bright as it had ever been, burning them both where they sat.

Her gaze was like a touch on his, and he felt it everywhere. "I have a different theory."

"I'm all ears, of course. Every inmate is innocent, every killer was merely misunderstood, every con man an

artist in his soul, et cetera. Tell me your sob story, *cara*."
He felt his mouth crook. "I knew you would, sooner or
later."

But Paige only smiled, and her eyes were so green tonight they rivaled his own lush fields. It moved in him
like summer, an exultation of all that boundless heat that
spiked the air between them.

"You don't want revenge. Not really. You want sex."

Her smile deepened when he only stared back at her,
that mouth of hers still an utter distraction, still his undoing. Her gaze proud and unwavering and he had no
defense against that, either.

"You don't want to admit it, given what happened the
last time we had sex, but look where we are." She lifted
a shoulder, somehow encompassing the whole of the estate in that simple little gesture. "You've made sure there
couldn't possibly be a camera here. You've cut us off
from the rest of the world. And you're calling it *revenge*
because you're furious that you still want me."

"Or because *wanting* you is only part of it," he replied,
stiffer than he should have sounded, because it was that
or let loose the wild thing in him that wanted nothing but
her however he could have her. That didn't give a toss
about the rest of it as long as he got his hands on her one
more time. Just one more time. "And not mutually exclusive with revenge, I assure you."

Her smile seemed to pierce straight through him
then, heat and fire and danger, and it sank straight to
his sex.

Making him nothing at all but that wildness within.

"Call it whatever you want," she suggested in that
rough voice of hers that hinted at her own dark excitement, that called to him like a song the way it always had.
That sang in him still, no matter how he tried to deny it.

"Call it *hate sex*. I don't care, Giancarlo." She shrugged. "Whatever it is, whatever you need to call it to feel better about it, I want it, too."

"I beg your pardon?" Giancarlo's voice was a rough whisper that somehow sounded in Paige like a bellow.

It was the wine, Paige told herself as she stared back at him, her own words seeming to cavort between them on the heavily laden tabletop, making it impossible to see or hear much of anything else. Of course it was the wine—though she'd only had a few sips—and the lingering jet lag besides, though she didn't feel anything like tired at the moment.

Nothing else could possibly have made her say such things, she was sure, much less throw down the gauntlet to a battle she very much feared might be the end of her.

She opened her mouth to take it back, to laugh and claim she'd been kidding, to break the strange, taut spell that stretched between them and wrapped them tight together, caught somewhere in that arrested expression that transformed his beautiful face. But Giancarlo lifted an aristocratic hand that stopped her as surely as if he'd placed it over her mouth, and she knew she really shouldn't have shivered in a rush of dark delight at the very image.

"I find I'm not as trusting as I used to be," he told her, though *untrusting* wasn't how she would have described the wolfish look in his dark eyes then. "It is a personality flaw, I am sure. But I'm afraid you'll have to offer proof."

She was watching his mouth as if it was a show, which was only part of the reason Paige didn't understand what he'd said. She blinked. "Proof?"

"That this is not another one of your dirty little games

that will end up painting the front page of every godfor-saken gossip rag in existence." He lounged back in his chair, but his eyes were hot, and she had the notion that he was coiled to strike. "You understand my reticence, I'm sure."

"And I'd offer you my word," she said, not sure how she kept her tone so light, as if *dirty little games* hadn't pricked at her and hurt while it did, because he had no idea what kind of dirt she'd been drowning in back then, "but somehow, I'm betting that won't be enough for you."

"Sadly, no," he agreed. He sounded anything but sad. "Though it pains me to cast such aspersions on your char-acter, even if only by insinuation."

"Oh, that's what that look on your face is." Her tone was arch and if she hadn't known better, if she hadn't known it was impossible, she might have thought she was enjoying herself here. "It looks a bit more like glee than pain from this side of the table, I should tell you."

Giancarlo smiled, dark and intent. "I can't imagine why."

The night air seemed to shimmer in the space between them, in the flickering light of the candles and in the vel-vety dark that surrounded the table like an embrace. He settled even farther back in his chair and stretched his legs out again, like an indolent god awaiting a sacrifice, and Paige knew she should put a stop to this before it got out of control—but she didn't. The truth was she didn't want to stop it. She didn't want to do anything but this.

"Strip." It was a hoarse command, rich and dark, like the finest chocolate poured over her skin, and she should have been outraged by his arrogance. Instead, she wanted to bathe in it. In him.

Wasn't that always what she'd wanted?

She didn't pretend she hadn't heard him or that she didn't understand. "Here?"

"Right here." His dark gaze burned, gold and onyx, daring her. "Unless there is some new reason you refuse to obey me this time?"

"You mean, besides the fact that we're sitting outside? Where anyone could see us engaged in all manner of shocking acts? I thought you had a horror of public displays of anything."

"How shocking could a simple strip show be?" he asked, and there was something else in his gaze then, sharp and hard. "It has slipped your mind, perhaps, that the entire world has already seen us having sex. I doubt anything we do could possibly shock them now. Unless you've learned new tricks since I last saw you?"

"Nothing but the same old tricks here," she said, keeping her tone the same as it was, as if that slap of history hadn't made her feel dizzy at all. It was too bad nothing seemed to keep her from wanting him. She was that masochistic. "I'm sorry to disappoint you. Should I keep my clothes on?"

Paige saw that flash of fury in his gaze once more, but it melted into molten heat in the space of a heartbeat, as if they were both masochists here. Somehow, that made her feel better.

"No," he said in a low voice. "You most certainly should not."

"Then it seems I have no choice but to obey you, as promised," she said quietly. "Despite your poor, apparently unshockable neighbors and the things they might see."

"The closest resident aside from my mother is over forty miles away tonight," Giancarlo said, as if impatient. But she could see the fire in his gaze. She could practically taste his need. "Your modesty is safe enough, such as it is. What other excuses do you have?" He let out a bark of something not quite laughter. "We might as well address them all now and be done with them."

"What happens after I strip for you?" Paige asked, almost idly, but she was already pushing her chair back with a too-loud scrape against the stones, then rising to her feet. "This is daring, indeed, to get me naked and then leave me standing here all alone. Is that the plan? It's something of a waste, I'd think."

"First we'll worry about whatever cameras you might have secreted on that body of yours," he told her, and if she hadn't known him she might have thought him cold. Unmoved by all of this. But that wild, uninhibited lover she'd known lurked there in the sensual curve of his lips, that gleaming thing deep in his gaze. Giancarlo might hate her, but he wanted her as much as she did him. And Paige clung to that, perhaps harder than she should have. She clung to it as if it was everything and opted not to listen to the alarms that rang out in her at the thought. "Then we'll worry about what to do with that body."

"Whatever you say, Count Alessi," she murmured, which was as close to obedient as she'd ever come. She saw a certain appreciation for that—or for her wry tone, more like—in his dark eyes, but then it was time to dance.

Because that was what this was. Paige didn't pretend otherwise. The only music was his breath and hers, the only audience the primeval explosion of stars above them. She hadn't danced in years. Ten years, in fact. But she could feel him in her feet, in her hips. In the glorious stretch of her arms over her head. Her pulse and her breath. She could feel him everywhere, better than any sound track with her own hopeful heartbeat like the kick of drums, and she danced.

She poured herself into each undulation of her hips, each exultant reach of her hands. She'd kicked off her shoes when she'd stood and she curled her toes down hard into the smooth stones beneath her, feeling what was left of the day's heat against her soles and that wild-fire that only arced higher between the two of them as she moved. She tried her best to catch the sensation in the movement of her hips, her legs, her torso. She took her time peeling off her trousers, managing to kick them aside with a flourish, and then she moved closer to him as she rid herself of her shirt, as if his intent expression beckoned her to him.

She took her time with her bra, offering her breasts to him when she finally dropped it at her side, and she smiled at the way he moved in his chair, his gaze a wild touch on her skin, so fierce it made her nipples pull taut. And she wasn't done. She kept up the dance, the ecstatic dance, and she made it her apology, her regret. She told him all about her love and her silly, shattered hopes with every move she made, and when she stepped out of her panties she didn't know which one of them was breath-ing more heavily.

Paige only knew that he was standing, too. And that she was naked before him and she still wasn't done.

Naked in the Tuscan night, she danced for all those dreams she'd let carry her away as a girl. For the dream she'd destroyed with a single phone call and a cashed check ten years ago, and none of it worth the sacrifice, in the end. It was like skinny-dipping, warm and cool at once, the summer air a sensual caress against her flesh. She danced for the joy she'd only ever felt in this man's presence, the laughter she still missed, the love she'd squandered for good reasons that seemed nothing but sad in retrospect.

She danced and she danced, and she might have danced all night, but Giancarlo swept her into his arms instead, high against his chest, and that was like a much better dance. Hotter and more intense, and then his mouth came down on hers, claiming her and destroying her that easily.

He came down hard on top of her and she loved it. That lean, hard body of his crushing her with his delicious weight, his narrow hips keeping her legs apart, and it took her a moment to realize that he'd moved them over to one of the sun chaises that sat around the gleaming, sleek pool that jutted out from the loggia toward the vineyards. And that he'd lost his jacket in the move.

And he looked as gorgeously undone as she felt, and very nearly as wild.

"Giancarlo," she whispered, the dance still running madly in her veins, almost as addictive as he was. "Don't stop."

"I give the orders, not you," he growled, but his lips were curved when they took hers all over again.

And then everything slowed down. Turned to honey, thick and sweet.

Giancarlo feasted on her as if she were the gourmet meal his chefs had prepared for him, and beneath his talented mouth she felt almost that cherished, that perfect. She wanted his naked skin pressed to hers more than she could remember wanting anything else, ever, but he kept her too busy to peel his shirt back from his strong shoulders.

He kissed her until her head spun, and then he followed the line of her neck, tasting her and muttering dark things in Italian that she told herself she was happy she didn't understand.

Even if they moved in her like music, dark and compelling, sex and magic and *Giancarlo,* at long last.

He found her breasts and pulled one of the proud nipples deep into his hot mouth, and she didn't care what he *said.* Or in what language. She arched into him, mindless and needy, and he punished and praised her with his lips, his tongue, the scrape of his teeth. He played with her until she begged him to stop and then he only laughed and kept going, sending a catapult of pure wildfire straight down into her core.

She thought for a panicky, wondrous second that he might throw her straight over the edge with only this—

But he stopped, as diabolical as ever, raising his dark head to take in the flushed heat on her face and all down her neck. Her sensual distress. Her driving need.

"This punishment appears to be far more effective than you imagined it would be, *cara*," he murmured, his voice another sensual shiver against her sensitive skin, with its echoes of the playfully wicked lover she'd met so long ago. "It's almost as if you forgot what I can do to you."

"Thank you for the harsh lesson, Count Alessi," she whispered, not trying too hard to keep her tone anything approaching respectful when she was this close to the edge. "May I have another?"

He laughed, and she did too, and she didn't know if she'd been kidding or if she'd meant it when he returned his attention to her body, shifting to crawl down farther. If these were harsh lessons indeed, or gifts. He left a shimmering trail of fire from her breasts to her belly, and when he paused there, his breath fanning out over the hungriest part of her, Paige realized she was breathing as heavily as if she was running a race. The marathon he'd mentioned earlier, God help her.

"You'd better hold on," he warned her, dark and stirring and *right there* against her sex. "I'm going to stop when I'm done, not when you are."

And then he simply bent his head and licked his way into her.

Paige ignited.

She went from the mere sensation of burning straight into open flame. She couldn't seem to catch her breath. She arched against the exquisite torment of his wickedly clever mouth, or she tried to escape it, and either way, it didn't matter. He gripped her hips in his strong hands and he tasted her molten heat as if it was his own greatest pleasure, and before she knew it she was bucking against him, her hands buried deep in his thick, dark hair.

Calling out his name like a prayer into the night.

And he was as good as his word. He didn't stop. He didn't wait for her to come back down, to come back to herself. He simply kept on tasting her, settling in and taking his time, laughing against her tender flesh when she begged him to stop, laughing more when she begged him to keep on going.

The fire poured back into her, hotter and higher than before, and then he plunged two fingers deep inside of her and threw her over the side of the world. Again.

This time, when she shuddered her way back to earth, Giancarlo had moved off her to stand beside her, his hard hands impatient as he pulled her to her feet. It took her a moment to realize he'd finally stripped but she had no time to appreciate it, because he was lying back on the chaise and pulling her down to sit astride him.

"I want to watch," he told her, his voice dark and nearly grim with need, and it lit that flame inside of her all over again.

And then he simply curled his strong hands around her hips the way he had a thousand times before, the way she'd never dreamed he would again, and thrust home.

CHAPTER SIX

HE WAS INSIDE her again. At last.

Finally.

Giancarlo thought the sensation—far better than all his pale memories across these long years, far better than his own damned hand had ever been—might make him become a religious man.

She was so damned hot, molten and sweet and slick and *his,* and she still held him so tightly, so snugly, it was nearly his undoing. Her hair was that deep black ink with hints of fire and it tumbled all around her in a seductive tousle, falling to those breasts of hers, still high and pert, the tips already tight again and begging for his mouth.

Paige looked soft and stunned, exactly how he liked her best, exactly how he remembered her, and then she made everything better by reaching out to prop her hands against his chest. The shift in position made her sink down even farther on him, making them both groan.

He let his hands travel back to cup the twin globes of her delectable bottom, and tested the depth of her, the friction. God help him, but she was perfect. She had always been perfect. The perfect fit. The perfect fire.

Perfect for him.

Giancarlo had somehow forgotten that, in all the long years since he'd last been inside her. He'd convinced himself he'd exaggerated this as some kind of excuse for his own idiocy—that she'd been nothing more than a pretty girl with a dancer's body and all the rest had been a kind of madness that would make no sense if revisited.

But this was no exaggeration. This was pure, hot, bliss. This was that same true perfection he remembered, at last.

Paige looked down at him, her gaze unreadable. Bright and something like awed. And then she started to move.

He had watched her dance ten years ago, and he had wanted her desperately. He'd watched her dance tonight, that astonishing performance for him alone, equal parts sensual and inviting, and he'd thought he might die if he didn't find a way inside her. But nothing compared to *this* dance. Nothing came close.

She braced herself against him, her hands splayed wide over his pectoral muscles, while her hips set a lazy, shattering, insistent rhythm against his. And Giancarlo was lost.

He forgot about revenge. He forgot about their past. Her deceit, his foolish belief in her. All the terrible lies. The damned pictures themselves, grainy and humiliating. He lost his plans in the slide of her body against his, the sleek thrill that built in him with every rocking motion she made. Every life-altering stroke of the hardest part of him so deep, so very deep, in all of her soft heat.

"Make me come," he ordered her, in a stranger's deep growl. He saw her skin prickle at the sound of it, saw the way she pulled her lower lip between her teeth as if she was fighting back the same wave of sensation he was. "Make it good."

Not that it could be anything but good. Not that it ever had been. This was a magical thing, this wild, hot fire that was only theirs. He could feel it every time he sank within her. He knew it every time he pulled back. He felt it in the sure pace she set with her hips, the tight hold of her flesh against his. He wanted it to go on forever, the way he'd thought it would when he'd met her that first time.

The way it should have, that little voice that was still in love with her, that had never been anything but in love with her, whispered deep inside him.

But she was following his orders and this was no time for regrets. She moved against him, lush and lovely, her hips a sinuous dance, a well-cast spell of longing and lust and too many other things he refused to name. He'd thought he'd lost her forever and yet she was here, moving above him, her lovely body on display because he'd wanted it, holding him so deep inside her he couldn't tell where he ended and she began. He didn't want to know.

"Your wish is my command, my count," she teased him, her voice a husky little dream, and then she did something complicated with her hips and the world turned to flames all around them.

When he finally exploded, a bright rush of fire turned some kind of comet, rocketing over the edge of the night, he heard her call out his name.

And then follow him into bliss.

Giancarlo did not welcome reality when it reasserted itself.

Paige lay slumped over him, her face buried in his neck, while he was still deep inside of her. He opted not to think about how easy it was to hold her, or how she still seemed to have been crafted especially to fit in his arms, exactly this way. It took him much longer than it should have to get his breathing under control again. He held her the way a lover might, the way he always had before, and stared out over the top of her head at the faint lights on distant hills and the smear of starlight above.

He wished he didn't care about the past. More than that, he wished he could trust her the way he had once. He wished so many things, and yet all of the stars were fixed tonight, staring down at him from their cold positions, and he knew better.

Paige was an accident waiting to happen. He'd been caught up in that accident once—he wouldn't subject himself to it again. Even he wasn't foolish enough to walk into the same trap twice. No matter that it felt like glory made flesh to touch her again, like coming home after too long away.

He would learn to live without that, too. He had before.

She shifted against him, and he felt the brush of her lips over his skin and told himself it was calculated. That everything about her was calculated. There was no use remembering the afternoons they'd spent curled around each other in his huge bed surrounded by the Malibu sea. When she'd tasted him everywhere with her eyes closed, as if she couldn't help herself, as if her affection was as elemental as the ocean beyond his windows or the sky above and she had no choice but to sink into it with all of her senses.

That had been an act. This was an act. He needed to remember it.

But that didn't mean he couldn't enjoy the show.

"You've obviously been practicing," he said, to be horrible. To remind them both that this was here and now, not ten years back. "Quite a lot, I'd say, were I to hazard a guess."

He felt her tense against him, but almost thought he'd imagined it when she sat up a moment later, displaying her typical offhanded grace. And then she smiled slightly as she looked down at him.

"I was about to compliment you on the same thing," she said, a brittle sort of mischief and something else lighting up her gaze. "You must have slept with a thousand women to do that so well! My congratulations. Especially as I would have said there weren't ten women you could sleep with in a hundred miles, much less a thousand. The privileges of wealth, I presume?"

"You're hilarious." But he couldn't help the crook of his mouth. "I have them flown in from Rome, of course."

"Of course." She wrinkled her nose at him, and it was as dangerous as it had been earlier. It made him want things he knew he couldn't have. He couldn't have them, and more to the point, she couldn't give them. Hadn't he learned anything? "You realize, Giancarlo, that people might get the wrong idea. They might begin to think you're a playboy whore."

"They won't."

"Because you tell them so?" She shook her head, her expression serious though her mysterious eyes laughed at him. "I think that tactic only works with me. And not very well."

"Because," he said, his hands moving to her bottom again, then higher along the tempting indentation in her lovely back to tug her down to him, "a man is only a playboy whore when he appears to be having too much of a certain kind of uncontrolled fun in public. I can do all the same things in private and it doesn't count. Didn't you know?"

Her attention dropped to his mouth and he wanted it there. He was already hardening within her again and she shifted restlessly against him as if she encouraged it, making the fire inside him leap to new life that easily.

"It all counts," she breathed. "Or none of it does."

"Then I suppose that makes us all whores, doesn't

it?" he asked. He indulged himself and sank his hands deep into her hair, holding her head fast, as he tested the depth of her again and found her hotter around him. Wetter. Better, somehow, than before. That quickly, he was like steel. "But let's be clear. How many lovers have you taken in the last ten years?"

"Less than your thousand," she said, her voice a thin little thing, as her hips met his greedily. Deliciously. He grunted, and then pulled out to flip them around, coming down over her again and drawing her legs around his waist. He teased her heat with the tip of his hardness, and he didn't know what it was that drove him then, but he didn't let her pull him into her.

"How many?" he asked. He had no idea why he cared. He didn't care. He'd imagined it a thousand times and it scraped at him and it changed nothing either way. But he couldn't seem to stop. "Tell me."

Her eyes moved to his, then away, and they looked blue in the shadows. "What does it matter? Whatever number I pick, you'll think the worst of me."

"I already think the worst of you," he said, the way he might have crooned love words a lifetime ago, and he couldn't have said what he wanted here. To hurt her? Or himself? To make this all worse? Or was this simply his way of reminding them both who they were? "Why don't you try the truth?"

"None," she said, and there was an odd expression on her face as she said it. He might have called it vulnerable, were she someone else. "I told you there were no new tricks."

It took another beat for him to process that, and then something roared in him, a primal force that was like some kind of howl, and he thought he shook though he knew he held himself perfectly still.

"Is that a joke?" But he was whispering. He barely knew his own voice.

Her wide mouth twisted and her gaze was dark with something he didn't want to understand. Something that couldn't possibly be real.

"Yes," she said, her voice broken and fierce at once. "Ha ha, what a joke. I meant ten. Twenty. How many lovers do you imagine I've taken, Giancarlo? What number proves I'm who you think I am?"

He heard her voice break slightly as she asked the question, and a kind of ripple went through her lush body. He felt it. This time when she urged him into her, he went, slick and hard and even better than before, making him mutter a curse and press his forehead to hers. And he didn't have the slightest idea if this was his form of an apology, or hers.

"I don't care one way or the other," he lied, and he didn't want to talk about this any longer. He didn't want to revisit all those images he'd tortured himself with over the years. Because his sad little secret was that he'd never imagined her in prison, the way he'd told her he had. He'd imagined her wrapped around some other man exactly like this and he'd periodically searched the internet to see if he could find any evidence that she was out there somewhere, doing it with all that same joy and grace that had undone him.

And it had killed him, every time. It still killed him.

So he took it out on her instead, in the best way possible. He set a hard pace, throwing them headfirst into that raging thing that consumed them both, and he laughed against the side of her neck when she couldn't do anything but moan out her surrender.

He held on, building that perfect wildness all over again, making her thrash and keen, and when he thought he couldn't take it any longer he reached between them and pressed hard against the center of her need, making her shatter all around him.

And he rode her until he could throw himself into that shattering, too. Until he could forget the truth he'd heard in her voice when she'd told him there hadn't been anyone since him, because he couldn't handle that—or what he'd seen on her face that he refused to believe. *He refused.*

He rode her until he could forget everything but this. Everything but her. Everything they built between them in this marvelous fire.

Until he lost himself all over again.

"Violet is asking for you," Giancarlo said.

Paige had heard him coming from a long way off. First the Jeep, the engine announcing itself high on the hill and only getting louder as it wound its way down toward her cottage. Then the slam of the driver's door. The thud of the cottage's front door, and then, some minutes later, the slide of the glass doors that led out to where she sat, curled up beneath a graceful old oak tree with her book in her lap.

"That sounds like an accusation," she said mildly, putting her book aside. He stood on the terrace with his hands on his lean hips, frowning at her. "Of course she's asking for me. I'm her assistant. She might be on vacation here, but I'm not."

"She needs to learn how to relax and handle her own affairs," he replied, somewhat darkly. Paige climbed to her feet, brushing at the skirt she wore, and started toward him. It was impossible not feel that hunger at the sight of him, deep inside her, making her too warm, too soft.

"Possibly," she said, trying to concentrate on something, anything but the sensual spell he seemed to weave simply by existing. "But I'm not her therapist, I'm her personal assistant. When she learns how to relax and handle her own affairs, I'm out of a job."

Her heart set up its usual clatter at his proximity, worse the closer she got to him, and she didn't understand how that could still happen. They'd been here almost a week. It should have settled down by now. She should have started to grow immune to him, surely. After all, she already knew how this would end. Badly. Unlike the last time, when she'd been so blissfully certain it would be the one thing in her life that ended well, this time she knew better. Their history was like a crystal ball, allowing her to see the future clearly.

Maybe too clearly. Not that it seemed to matter.

She stopped when she was near him but not too near him, and felt that warm thing in the vicinity of her heart when he scowled. He reached over and tugged her closer, so he could land a hard kiss on her mouth. *Like a mark of possession,* she thought, *more than an indication of desire*—but she didn't care.

It deepened, the way it always deepened. Giancarlo muttered something and angled his head, and when he finally pulled back she was wound all around him and flushed and there was that deep male satisfaction stamped all over his face.

"Later," he told her, like a promise, as if she'd been the one to start this.

And in this past week, Paige had learned that she'd take this man any way she could have him. She imagined that said any number of unflattering things about her, but she didn't care.

"I might be busy later," she told him loftily.

He smiled that hard smile of his that made her ache,

and he didn't look particularly concerned. "I will take that chance."

And she would let him, she knew. Not because he told her to. Not because he was holding anything over her head. But because she was helpless before her own need, even though she knew perfectly well it would ruin her all over again....

Later, she told herself. *I'll worry about it later.*

Because *later* was going to be all the years she got to live through on the other side of this little interlude, when he was nothing but a memory all over again. And she wasn't delusional enough to imagine that there was any possibility that when this thing with Giancarlo ended he might permit her to remain with Violet, in any capacity. He was as likely to fall to his knees and propose marriage.

She moved around him and into the house then, not wanting him to read that epic bit of silliness on her face, when that notion failed to make her laugh at herself the way it should have. When it made everything inside of her clutch hopefully instead. *You are such a fool,* she chided herself.

But then again, that wasn't news.

Paige swept up her bag and hung it over her shoulder, then followed Giancarlo out to his Jeep. He climbed in and turned the key, and she clung to the handle on her side of the vehicle as he bumped his way up the old lane and then headed toward the *castello* in the distance.

It was another beautiful summer's day, bright and perfect with the olive trees a silvery presence on either side of the lane that wound through the hills toward Violet, and Paige told herself it was enough. This was enough. It was more than she'd ever imagined could happen with Giancarlo after what she'd done, and why did she want to ruin it with thoughts of *more*?

But the sad truth was, she didn't know how to be anything but greedy when it came to this man. She wanted all of him, not the parts of himself he doled out so carefully, so sparingly. Not when she could feel he kept so much of himself apart.

She'd woken the morning after that first night to find herself in his bed. Alone. He'd left her there without so much as a note, and she'd lectured herself about the foolishness of her hurt feelings. She'd told herself she should count herself lucky he hadn't tossed her out his front door at dawn, naked.

What she told herself and what she actually went right on feeling, of course, were not quite the same thing.

Modify your expectations, girl, she'd snapped at herself on the walk down the hill to her cottage. The birds had been singing joyfully, the sun had been cheerful against her face, she was in *Italy* of all places, and Giancarlo had made love to her again and again throughout the night. He could call it whatever he wanted. She would hold it in her battered little heart and call it what it had meant to her.

Because she hadn't lied to him. She hadn't touched another man since him, and she'd grown to accept the fact she never would. At first it had hurt too much. She'd seen nothing but Giancarlo—and more important, his back, on that last morning when he'd walked away from her rather than talk about what had happened, what she'd done. Then she'd started working for Violet and it had seemed as if Giancarlo was everywhere, in pictures, in emails, in conversation. Paige had had the very acute sense that so much as going out to dinner with another man was some kind of treason—which she'd known was absurd. Beyond absurd, given the way in which she'd betrayed him. She'd made certain he hated her. He'd walked away from her without a single backward glance. Why should he care what she did?

And yet somehow, each of these ten years had crept by and he was still the only man she'd ever slept with. She'd been unable to contain the small, humming thing inside her then as that thought had kept her company on her walk. It had felt a little bit too much like a kind of silly joy she ought to have known better than to indulge.

But he'd turned up that night, his face drawn as if he'd fought a great battle with himself, and he hadn't seemed interested in talking about whether he'd lost or won. He'd led her up her stairs, thrown her on her bed, and kept them up for another night—this time, she'd noted, with the condoms they'd failed to use before.

They hadn't talked about that first night and its lack of birth control. Just like ten years ago, they hadn't talked about a thing.

And that was how it had been since her arrival, Paige thought now, as they drew closer to the *castello*. She'd never spent much time wondering what it felt like to be a rich man's *kept woman* before now. What she thought people in this part of the world might call a *mistress*. But she imagined it must be something like this past week.

Nothing but the pleasures of their flesh. No unpleasant topics, save the odd bout of teasing that never quite landed a hard punch. Nothing but sex and food and sex again, until she felt glutted on it. Replete. Able to know him at a touch, taste him when he wasn't there, scent him on any breeze.

The last time she'd felt so deeply a part of her own body, her own physical space, she'd been dancing more hours of the day than she'd slept.

She didn't tell him that, either. That she filled these golden, blue-skied days with dancing, as if the first dancing she'd done on that initial night with him had freed her. Paige hadn't understood how lost she'd been until she found herself out in the field near her cottage, dancing in great, wide circles beneath the glorious Tuscan sky with tears running down her face and her arms stretched toward the sun. She wanted nothing more than to share that with him.

But Giancarlo drove the Jeep with the same ferocity he did everything else—except in bed, where he indulged every sense and took his sweet time—and with that same hard edge of his old dark fury beneath it.

Almost as if he, too, preferred the little fairy tale they'd been living this past week, where she existed purely to please him, and did, again and again.

Paige knew better than to ask him about it. Or to tell him the things that moved in her, sharp and sweet, in this place that felt more like home every day. This was a no-talking zone. This was a place of sun and sex and silence. It was the only possible way it could work.

Like all temporary things, all stolen moments, it could only be a secret, or it would implode.

"What have you been up to all this time?" Violet asked, peering at Paige from her position on one of the *castello*'s lovely couches, her iPad in her lap and her voice no more than mildly reproving. "I thought perhaps you'd been sucked into one of the olive groves, never to be seen again."

"You should have told me you needed me!" Paige exclaimed instead of answering the question. Because she didn't want to know what Violet would think about the help touching her son. She didn't want to risk her relationship with either one of them. "I thought I was giving you some much-needed time and space to yourself!"

"My dear girl," Violet said, sounding amused, "if I

wanted time and space to myself, I would have chosen a different life altogether."

Paige was too aware of Giancarlo's dark, brooding presence on the other side of the living room then, lounging there against the massive stone fireplace, supposedly scrolling through his phone's display. She was certain he was hanging on every word. Or did she simply want to be that important to him?

There was no answer to that. Not one that came without a good dose of pain in its wake.

"I'm here now," Paige said stoutly, trying to focus on the woman who had always been good to her, without all these complications and regrets. *Not that she'd give you the time of day if she knew who you really were,* that rough voice that was so much like her mother's snarled at her.

"Then I have two questions for you," Violet replied, snapping Paige back to the present. "Can you operate a manual transmission?"

That hadn't been what Paige was expecting, but that was Violet. Paige rolled with it. "I can."

It was, in fact, one of the few things she could say her mother had taught her. Even if it had been mostly so that Paige could drive the beat-up car she owned to pick her up, drunk and belligerent, from the rough bars down near the railroad tracks.

"And do you want to drive me to Lucca?" Violet smiled serenely when Giancarlo made an irritated sort of noise from the fireplace across the room and kept her eyes trained on Paige. "If memory serves, it has wonderful shopping. And I'm in the mood for an adventure."

"An adventure with attention or without?" Paige asked without missing a beat, though she was well aware it had been a long time since Violet had gone out on one of her excursions into the public without expecting attention from the people who would see her out and about.

"Without," Giancarlo snapped, from much closer by, and Paige had to control a little jump. She hadn't heard him move.

"With, of course," Violet said, as if he hadn't spoken. "No one has fawned over me in a whole week, and I require attention the way plants require sunlight, you know. It's how I maintain my youthful facade."

She said it as if she was joking, but in that way of hers that didn't actually allow for any argument. Not that it was Paige's place to argue. Her son, however, was a different story.

"You're one of the most famous women in the world," Giancarlo pointed out, and the dark thing Paige heard in his voice was a different animal than the one he used when he spoke to her. More exasperated, perhaps. Or more formal. "It's not safe for you to simply wander the streets alone."

"I won't be alone. I'll have Paige," Violet replied.

"And what, pray, will Paige do should you find yourself surrounded? Mobbed?" Giancarlo rolled his eyes. "Hold the crowd off with a smart remark or two?"

"I wouldn't underestimate the power of a smart remark," Paige retorted, glaring at him—but his gaze was on his mother.

"That was a long time ago," Violet said softly. With a wealth of compassion that made Paige stiffen in surprise and Giancarlo jerk back as if she'd slapped him. "I was a very foolish young woman. I underestimated the kind of interest there would be—not only in me, but in you. Your father was livid." She studied her son for a moment and then rose to her feet, smiling faintly at Paige. "We were in the south of France and I thought it would be a marvelous idea to go out and poke around the shops by myself. Giancarlo was four. And when the crowds surrounded us, he was terrified."

"The police were called," he said, furiously, Paige thought, though his voice was cold. "You had to be rescued by armed officials and you never went out without security again—and neither did I. I hope you haven't spent your life telling this story as if I was an overimaginative child who caused a fuss. It wasn't a monster in my closet. It was a pack of shouting cameramen and a mob of fans."

"The point is, my darling, you were four," Violet said quietly. "You are not four any longer. And while I flatter myself that I remain relevant, I am an old woman who has not commanded the attention of packs of paparazzi in a very long time. I'm perfectly capable of enjoying an afternoon with my assistant and, if you insist, *one* driver."

"And you wonder why I refuse to have children," he growled at her, and it took every shred of self-preservation Paige had to keep from reacting to that. To Giancarlo and the pain she could hear beneath the steel in his voice. "Why I would die before I'd subject another innocent to this absurd world of yours."

"I didn't wonder," Violet replied. "I knew. But I hoped you'd outgrow it."

"Mother—"

"I don't like being locked away in Italian castles, Giancarlo," she said, and there was steel in the way she said it, despite the smile she used. It was the famous star issuing a command, not a mother. "If you cast your memory back, you'll remember that I never have."

There was a strange tension in the room then. And though she knew better, though it would no doubt raise the suspicions of the woman who could read anyone,

standing right there beside her, Paige found herself looking to Giancarlo as if she could soothe him somehow. As
if he'd let her—

And she found that great darkness blazing in his eyes
as he slowly, slowly turned his attention from Violet to
her.

As if this was something she'd done, too.

Because, of course, she had. When he'd been far older
than four. And what she'd done to him hadn't been an
accident.

The truth of that almost knocked her sideways, and
she would never know how she remained standing. She
wanted to tell him everything, and who cared what Violet thought? She wanted to explain about her mother's
downward spiral. The money owed, the threats from the
horrible Denny, the fear and panic that she'd thought
were just the way life was. Because that was how it had
always been. Paige wanted him to understand—at last—
that she never, ever would have sacrificed him if she
hadn't believed she had no other choice. If she hadn't
been trapped and terrified herself, with only hideous
options on all sides.

But this wasn't the place and she knew—*she knew*—
he wouldn't want to hear it anyway. He didn't want to
know *why*. He only wanted her to pay.

He didn't realize that she had. That she still did. Every
moment since.

And so she stood there, she said nothing the way she'd
always said nothing and somehow she managed not to
fall to her knees. Somehow Paige managed not to break
into pieces. Somehow, she stared back at him as if she'd
never broken his heart and she wished, hard and fierce
and utterly pointless, that it were true.

"Don't worry," he said quietly, as if he was answering

his mother. All of that darkness in his gaze. All of the betrayal, the loss. The terrible grief. It made Paige's chest ache, so acutely that she forgot to worry that Violet would be able to sense it from a few feet away. So sharp and so deep she thought it might have been a mortal blow, and how could anyone hide that? "I remember everything."

CHAPTER SEVEN

LUCCA WAS A walled city, an old fortress turned prosperous market town, and it was enchanting. Paige dutifully followed Violet through the bustle of tiled red roofs, sloped streets and the sheer tumult of such an ancient place, and told herself there was no reason at all she should feel so unequal to the task she'd done so well and well-nigh automatically for years.

But her heart wasn't with her in the colorful city. It was back in the hills with the man she'd left there, with that look on his face and too much dark grief in his gaze.

And the longer Violet lingered—going in and out of every shop, pausing for cell phone photos every time she was recognized, settling in for a long dinner in a restaurant where the chef came racing out to serenade her and she was complimented theatrically for her few Italian phrases, all while Paige looked on and/or assisted—the more Paige wondered if the other woman was doing it deliberately. As if she knew what was going on between her son and her assistant.

But that was impossible, Paige kept telling herself.

This is called guilt, that caustic voice inside her snapped as Violet flirted outrageously with the chef. *This is why you're here. Why you work for his mother. Why you accept how he treats you. You deserve it. You earned it.*

More than that, she missed him. One afternoon know-ing Giancarlo wasn't within reach, that there was no chance he'd simply appear and tumble her down onto the nearest flat surface, the way he'd done only yester-day with no advance warning, and she was a mess. If this was a preview of what her life was going to be like after this all ended, Paige thought as she handled Violet's bill and called for the car, she was screwed.

"Like that's anything new," she muttered under her breath as she climbed into the car behind Violet, nearly closing the heavy door on the still-grasping hands of the little crowd that had gathered outside the restaurant to adore her.

"Pardon?" Violet asked.

Paige summoned her smile. Her professional de-meanor, which she thought she'd last seen weeks ago in Los Angeles. "Did that do? Scratch the attention itch?"

"It did." Violet sat across from her in the dark, her gaze out the window as the car started out of the city. "Giancarlo is a solitary soul. He doesn't understand that some people recharge their batteries in different ways than he does. Not everyone can storm about a lonely field and feel recharged."

Said the woman who had never passed a crowd she couldn't turn into a fan base with a few sentences and a smile. Paige blinked, amazed at her churlishness even in her own head, and found Violet's calm gaze on hers.

"You're an extrovert." Paige said evenly. "I'm sure he knows that by now. Just as he likely knows that therefore, his own needs are different from yours."

"One would think," Violet agreed in her serene, untrou-bled way, which shouldn't have sent a little shiver of warn-ing down Paige's back. "But then, the most interesting men are not always in touch with what they need, are they?"

Violet didn't speak much after that, yet Paige didn't feel as if she could breathe normally until the car pulled off the country road and started along the winding drive into the estate. And she was impatient—the most impatient she'd ever been in Violet's presence, though she tried valiantly to disguise it—as she helped the older woman into the *castello* and oversaw the staff as they sorted out her purchases.

And only when she was finally in the car again and headed toward her cottage did Paige understand what had been beating at her all day, clutching at her chest and her throat and making her want to scream in the middle of ancient Italian piazzas. Guilt, yes, but that was a heavy thing, a spiked weight that hung on her. The rest of it was panic.

Because any opportunity Giancarlo had to reflect on what was happening between them—not revenge, not the comeuppance he'd obviously planned—was the beginning of the end. She knew it, deep inside. She'd seen it in his eyes this morning.

And when she got to her cottage and found not only it but the house above it dark, it confirmed her fears.

Paige stood there in the dark outside her cottage long after the driver's car disappeared into the night, staring up the hill, willing this shadow or that to separate from the rest and become Giancarlo. She was too afraid to think about what might happen if this was it. If that kiss he'd delivered in the garden was their last.

Too soon, she thought desperately, or perhaps that was the first prayer she'd dared make in years. *It's too soon.*

She stared up the side of the hill as if that would call him to her, somehow. But the only thing around her was the soft summer night, pretty and quiet. Still and empty, for miles around.

When she grew too cold and he still didn't appear, she made her way inside, feeling more punished by his absence than by anything else that had happened between them. Paige entertained visions of marching up the hill and taking what she wanted, or at least finding him and seeing for herself what had happened in her absence today, but the truth was, she didn't dare. She was still so uncertain of her welcome.

Would he throw back the covers and yank her into his arms if she appeared at his bedside? Or would he send her right back out into the night again, with a cruel word or two as her reward? Paige found she was too unsure of the answer to test it.

There were red flags everywhere, she acknowledged as she got ready for bed and crawled beneath her sheets. Red flags and dark corners, and nothing safe. But maybe what mattered was that she knew that, this time. She'd known the moment she'd decided to apply for that job with Violet. She'd always known.

She would have to learn to live with that, too.

Later that night, Paige woke with a sudden start when a lean male form crawled into her bed, hauling her into his arms.

Giancarlo. Of course.

But her heart was already crashing against her ribs as he rolled so she was beneath him. Excitement. Relief. The usual searing hunger, sharper than usual this time.

"Why didn't you come to me?" he gritted at her, temper and need and too many other dark and hungry things in his voice. Then the scrape of his teeth against the tender flesh of her neck, making her shudder.

Paige didn't want to think about the contours of her fears now, her certainty he'd finished with this. With her. Not now, while he was braced above her, his body so familiar and hot against hers, making the night blaze with the wild need that was never far beneath the surface. Never far at all.

Not even when she thought she'd lost him again.

"I thought you'd gone to bed already." *I didn't know if you'd want me to come find you,* she thought, but wisely kept to herself. "All of your lights were out."

She thought she saw a certain self-knowledge move over his face then, but it was gone so quickly she was sure she must have imagined it.

"Did you have a lovely day out with my mother?" he asked in a tone she wasn't foolish enough to imagine was friendly, his dark eyes glittering in the faint light from the rising moon outside her windows. "Filled with her admirers, exactly as she wished?"

"Of course." Paige ran her hands from his hard jaw to the steel column of his neck, as if trying to imprint the shape of him on her palms. Trying to make certain that if this was the last time, she'd remember it. That it couldn't be snatched from her, not entirely. "When Violet decrees we are to have fun, that is precisely what we have. No mere crowd would dare defy the crown jewel of the Hollywood establishment."

Giancarlo didn't laugh. He shifted his body so he was hard against her and she melted the way she always did, ready to welcome him no matter his mood or hers, no matter the strange energy that crackled from him tonight, no matter the darkness that seemed wrapped around him even as he wound himself around her.

There were other words for what she was with this man, she knew, words she hadn't heard in a long time but still remembered all too well. Words she'd dismissed as the unhealthy rantings of the worst person she'd ever known, the person who had taken everything she'd wanted from her—but it turned out dismissing them wasn't the same thing as erasing them.

Even so, the hollow, gnawing thing that had sat inside her all day and made her feel so panicked was gone, because he was here. She filled it with his scent, his touch, his bold possession.

Him. Giancarlo.

The only man she'd ever touched. The only man she'd ever loved.

And this was the only way she could tell him any of that. With her body. Paige shifted so he was flush against her entrance and hooked her legs over his hips, letting him in. Loving him in the only way she knew. In the only way he'd let her.

"Maybe that didn't always work out when you were a child," she whispered, hoping he couldn't read too much emotion in her eyes, across her face. "But my relationship with Violet is much easier. She pays, I agree, the end."

Giancarlo bent his head to press hot, open kisses along the ridge of her collarbone. Paige moved restlessly, hungrily against him, tilting her head back to give him greater access. To give him anything—everything—he wanted.

Because this won't last forever, that harsh voice that was too much an echo of her mother's reminded her. That was what today had taught her. There were no fairy tales. This situation had an expiration date, and every moment she had with him was one moment closer to the end.

"In a way," Giancarlo said, still too dark, still too rough, his mouth against her skin so Paige could feel the rumble of his words inside of her as he spoke, "that is every relationship that Violet has."

She heard that same tense grief that had been in him in the *castello* that morning and this time, no one was watching. She could soothe him, or try. She ran her fingers through his thick hair and smiled when he pressed into her touch, like a very large cat.

"I don't think it can be easy to be a great figure," Paige said after a moment, concentrating on the feel of his scalp beneath her fingertips, the drag of his thick hair as she moved her hands through it, the exquisite sensation of stroking him. "Too many expectations. Too much responsibility to something far bigger than oneself. The constant worry that it will be taken away. But it must be harder still to be that person's child."

He shifted away from her, propping himself up on his elbows, though he kept himself cradled there between her thighs, his arousal a delicious weight against her softness. A promise. The silence stretched out and his face was in shadow, so all she could see was the glitter of his dark gold eyes, and the echo of it deep inside her.

"It's not hard," he said, and she'd never heard that tone before, had she? Clipped and resigned at once. And yet somehow, that pit in her belly yawned open again as he spoke. "As long as you remember that she is always playing a role. The *grande dame* as benevolent mother. The living legend as compassionate parent. The great star whose favorite role of all is *mom*. When she was younger there were different roles threaded into the mix, but the same principle applied. You learn this as a child in a thousand painful ways and you vow, if you are at all wise, never to inflict it on another. To let it end with you."

Paige tried to imagine Giancarlo as a small boy, all stubborn chin and fathomless eyes, and ached for him, though that didn't explain her nervousness. It was something in the way he held himself apart from her, a certain danger rippling down the length of his body, as hard and as steel-hewn as he was. It was the way he watched her, too still, too focused.

"I'm sorry," she said, though she wanted to say so much more. She didn't dare. Just like before, when she'd stood outside and wanted him and had known better than to go and find him, she was too uncertain. "That can't have been easy."

"Is that sympathy for me, *cara*? Don't bother."

He wasn't quite scoffing at her. Not quite, though his face went fierce in the darkness, edging toward cruel the way he'd been in the beginning, and she found she was bracing herself—unable to open her mouth and stop him. Unable to defend herself at all. *Whatever he's about to say,* that hard voice reminded her, like another slap, *you deserve.*

"Here is what I learned from my mother, the great actress," Giancarlo said. "That she is a mystery, unknowable even to herself. That she prefers it that way. That intimacy is anathema to her because it cannot be controlled, it cannot be directed, it cannot cut to print when she is satisfied with her performance. It is one long take with no rehearsal and no do-overs, and she goes to great lengths indeed to avoid it."

Paige wasn't sure why she felt so stricken then, so stripped raw when he wasn't talking about her—but then he moved again, dropping his weight against her to whisper in her ear, hot and close and dark. So very dark.

You deserve this, she told herself. *Whatever it is.*

"I want a woman I can trust, *Paige*," he said with a ruthless inevitability. And it didn't even hurt. It was like a deep slice of a sharp blade. She knew he'd cut her and now there was only the wait for blood. For the pain that would surely follow. And he wasn't finished. "A woman I can know inside and out. A woman who carries no secrets, who does not hide herself away from me or from the world, who never plays a role. A woman who wants a partner, not an audience."

"Giancarlo." She felt torn apart even though he was holding her close. Wrecked as surely as if he'd thrown her from the roof of the towering *castello*. "Please."

But the worst part was, he knew what he was doing. She'd seen it in the cast of his sensual mouth. She'd felt it in the way he'd very nearly trembled as he'd held himself above her.

He knew he was hurting her. And he kept going.

"I want a woman I can believe when she tells me she loves me," he said, raw and fierce and she knew she deserved that, she knew she did, even though it felt a little bit like dying. And then he lifted his head to look her straight in the eyes, making it that much worse. "And that can never be you, can it? It never was. It never will be."

Later, she thought she might take that apart and live awhile in the misery he'd packed into those last two sentences. Later, she thought she might cry for days and check herself for scars, the way she'd done ten years ago. But that was later.

Tonight Paige thought the pain in him was far greater than the hurt he'd caused—that she deserved, that voice kept telling her, and she agreed no matter how it cut her up—and she couldn't bear it.

She didn't care if he still hated her, even now, after another week in his bed when he'd tasted every part of her and had to have recognized the sheer honesty in her response to him. She told herself she didn't care about that at all and some part of her believed it.

Or wanted to believe it.

But worrying about that was for later, too. Later, when she could put herself together again. Later, when she

could think about something other than the man who
stretched over her and broke her heart, again and again
and again. Because he could.

"Giancarlo," she said again, with more force this time.
"Stop talking."

And he surrendered with a groan, thrusting deep and
hard inside of her where there was nothing but the two of
them—that shimmering truth that was only theirs, wild
and dizzying and hotter every time—and that perfect,
wondrous fire that swept them both away in its glory.

And Paige did her best to make them both forget.

Two more weeks passed, slow and sweet. The Tuscan
summer started to edge toward the coming fall. The air
began to feel crisp in the mornings, and the sky seemed
bluer. And if she'd allowed herself to think about such
things, Paige might have believed that the tension between her and Giancarlo was easing, too—all that heavy
grief mellowing, turning blue like the sky, gold like the
fields, lighter and softer with age.

Or perhaps she'd taught them both how to forget.

Whatever it was, it worked. No more did she spend
her days trapped in her isolated cottage, available only
to him and only when he wanted—and she told herself
she didn't miss it, all that forced proximity and breathlessness. Of course she didn't miss it.

Paige's days looked a great deal as they had back
home. She met with Violet most mornings, and helped
her plan out her leisure time. Violet was particularly fond
of day trips to various Italian cities to soak in all the art
and culture and fashion with a side helping of adula-
tion from the locals, which she often expedited by taking Giancarlo's helicopter that left from the roof of the

castello and kicked up such a ruckus when it returned it could be heard for miles around.

"I've always preferred a big entrance," Violet had murmured the first time, that famous smile of hers on her lips as the helicopter touched down.

But when Violet was in between her trips—which meant days of spa treatments and dedicated lounging beneath artfully placed umbrellas at the side of the *castello*'s private pool instead—Paige was left to her own devices, which usually meant she was left to Giancarlo's.

One day he stopped the Jeep the moment it was out of sight of the *castello*'s stout tower and knelt down beside the passenger door, pulling her hips to his mouth and licking his way into Paige right there—making her sob out his name into the quiet morning, so loud it startled the birds from the nearby trees. Another time he drove them out to one of the private lakes that dotted the property and they swam beneath the hot sun, then brought each other to a shuddering release in the shallow end, Giancarlo holding her to him as she took advantage of the water's buoyancy to make him groan.

Other times, they talked. He told her of his father's dreams for this land, its long history and his own plans to monetize it while conserving it, that it might last for many more generations. He showed her around the Etruscan ruins that cropped up in the oddest spots and demonstrated, as much as possible, that a man who knew the ins and outs of three thousand acres in such extraordinary detail seemed something like magical when the landscape in question was a woman's body. *Her* body.

Paige didn't know which she treasured more. His words or his body. But she held them to her like gifts, and she tried not to think about what she deserved, what she knew she had coming to her. She tried to focus on what she had in her hands, instead.

One lazy afternoon they lay together in the warm sun, the sweet breeze playing over their heated skin. Paige propped her chin against his chest and looked into his eyes and it was dizzying, the way it was always dizzying. And then he smiled at her without a single stray shadow in his gorgeous eyes, and it was as if the world slammed to a stop and then started in the other direction.

"I saw you dancing in the garden the other night," he said.

There was no reason to blush. She told herself the heat she felt move over her was the sun, the leftover fire of the way he'd torn her to pieces only moments before, and nothing more.

"I haven't danced in a long while," she said, and she wanted to tear her gaze away from his, but she didn't. Or she couldn't. He ran his hand through her hair, slow and sweet, and she was afraid of the things he could see in her. And so afraid of the things she wanted.

"Why not?"

And Paige didn't know how to answer that. How to tell him the why of it without blundering straight into all the land mines they'd spent these weeks avoiding. That they'd managed to avoid entirely after that night she'd come back late from Lucca.

I want a woman I can trust, he'd said, and she wanted him to trust her. She might not deserve his trust, but she wanted it.

"I was good," she said after a moment, because that was true enough, "but I wasn't *amazing.* And there were so many other dancers who were as good as I was, but wanted it way more than I did."

Especially after he'd left and she hadn't had the heart

for it any longer, or anything else involving the body she'd used to betray the one man she'd ever given it to. She'd auditioned for one more gig and her agent had told her they'd said it was like watching a marionette. That had been her last audition. Her last dance, period.

Because once she'd lost Giancarlo, she'd lost interest in the only other thing she'd had that'd ever had any meaning in her life. Her mother had descended even further into that abyss of hers and Paige had simply been *lost*. And when she'd run into a woman she'd met through Giancarlo on one of those Malibu weekends, who'd needed a personal assistant a few days a week and had kind of liked that Paige was a bit notorious, it had seemed like a good idea. And more, a way to escape, once and for all, the dark little world her mother lived in.

A year later, she'd been working for a longtime television star who had no idea that competent Paige Fielding was related to *that* Nicola Fielding. A few years after that, she had enough experience to sign with a very exclusive agency that catered to huge stars like Violet, and when Violet's previous assistant left her, to put herself forward as a replacement. All of those things had seemed so random back then, as they happened. But now, looking back, it seemed anything but. As if Paige's subconscious had plotted out the only course that could bring her back to Giancarlo.

But she didn't want to think about that now. Or about what she'd do when she was without him again. How would she re-create herself this time? Where would she go? It occurred to her then that she'd never really planned beyond Violet. Beyond the road she'd known would bring her back to him.

I want a partner, he'd said, and the problem was, she

was a liar. A deliberate amnesiac, desperate to keep their past at bay. That wasn't a partner. That was a problem.

Giancarlo was still smiling, as if this was an easy conversation, and Paige wished it was. For once, *just once,* she wanted something to be as easy as it should have been.

"I'm surprised," he said, and there was something very much like affection in his gaze, transforming his face until he looked like that younger version of himself again. She told herself that it didn't make her ache. That it didn't make her heart twist tight. "I would have said dancing was who you were, not something you did."

"I was twenty years old," she heard herself say, in a rueful sort of tone that suggested an amusement she didn't quite feel. "I had no idea who I was."

You're his toy, Nicola, her mother had screamed at her in those final, dark days, when Paige had believed she'd somehow navigate her way through it all unscathed—that she'd manage to keep Giancarlo, please her mother and her mother's terrible friends, and pay off all of that debt besides. *He'll play with you until he's done and then he'll leave you broken and useless when he moves on to the next dumb whore. Don't be so naive!*

Giancarlo's face changed then, and his hand froze in her hair. "I think I always forget you were so young," he said after a moment, as if remembering her age shocked him. "What the hell was I doing? You were a kid."

She laughed then. She couldn't help it.

"My life wasn't exactly pampered and easy before I came to Hollywood," she told him, knowing as she said it that she'd never talked about that part of her life. He had been so bright, so beautiful—why would she talk about dark, grim things? "And I did that about ten minutes after I graduated from high school. My mom had the car packed and waiting on the last day of classes."

She shook her head at him as her laughter faded. "I was never really much of a kid."

She hadn't had the opportunity to be a kid, which wasn't quite the same thing, but she didn't tell him that. Even though she had the strangest idea that his childhood hadn't been that different from hers, really. The trappings couldn't have been more opposite, but she'd spent her whole life tiptoeing around, trying to predict what mood her mother would be in, how much she might have drunk, and how bad she could expect it to get of an evening. She wasn't sure that was all that different from trying to gauge one of Violet's moods.

It had never occurred to her that she'd traded one demanding mother for another, far classier one—and she wasn't sure she liked the comparison. *At least Violet cares for you in return,* she told herself then. *Which is more than Arleen ever did.*

"I'm not sure that excuses me," Giancarlo was saying, but then he laughed, and everything else shot straight out of her head and disappeared into that happy sound. "But then, I never had any control where you were concerned."

"Neither did I," she said, smiling at him, and they both stilled then. Perhaps aware in the same instant that they were straying too close to the very things they couldn't let themselves talk about.

Or the words they couldn't say. Words he'd told her he wouldn't believe if she did dare speak them out loud.

But that didn't keep her from feeling them. Nothing could.

He studied her face for a long moment, until she began to feel the breeze too keenly on her exposed skin. Or maybe that was her vulnerability. Having sex was much easier, for all it stripped her bare and seemed to involve every last cell in her body. It required only feeling and action. *Doing*. It was this *talking* that was killing her, making her want too much, making her imagine too many happy endings when, God help her, she knew better.

Paige pushed away from him, not willing to ruin this with a conversation that could only lead to more hurt. Or worse, something good that would be that much harder to leave behind when the time came. She sat up and gathered her clothes to her, pulling the flirty little sundress over her head as if the light material was armor. But she only wished it was.

"Was it ever real?" he asked quietly.

Paige didn't ask him what he meant. She froze, her eyes on the rolling hills that spread out before her in the afternoon light, the glistening lake in the valley below. That stunning Tuscan sky studded with chubby white clouds, the vineyards and the flowers, and she didn't think he understood that he was holding her heart between his palms and squeezing tight. Too tight.

Maybe he wouldn't care if he did.

"It was for me," she said, and her voice was too rough. Too dark. Too much emotion in it. "It always was for me, even at the end."

She didn't know what might happen then. What Giancarlo might say. Do. She felt spread open and hung out in all the open space around them, as if she was stretched across some tightrope high in the sky, subject to the whims of any passing wind—

His hand reached out and covered hers and he squeezed. Once.

And then he pulled on his clothes and he got to his feet and he never mentioned it again.

Giancarlo watched her sleep, and he did not require the chorus of angry voices inside of him to remind him that this was a bad idea.

He didn't know what had woken him, only that he'd come alert in a rush and had turned to make sure she was still there beside him—the way he'd done for years after the photographs hit. He'd lost count long ago of the number of times he'd dreamed it all away, dreamed she'd never betrayed him, dreamed that things had been different. He'd grown uncomfortably well used to lying there in his empty bed, glaring at the ceiling and wishing her ill even as he'd wanted her back, wherever she was.

But this time, she was right here. She was curled up beside him and sound asleep, so that she didn't even murmur when he stretched out on his side, his front to her back, and held her there. The way he knew he wouldn't do if she was awake, lest it give her too many ideas...

So much for your revenge plot, he chided himself, but it all seemed so absurd when she was lying beside him, her features taking on an angelic cast in the faint light that poured in from the skylight above them, the stars themselves lighting her with that special glow.

He found himself tracing the line of her cheek with his finger, the memories of ten years ago so strong he could almost have sworn that no time had passed. That the pictures and the separation had been the bad dream. Because he might be wary of her, but every day it seemed that was only because he thought he should be, not because he truly was. And every day it seemed to make less and less sense.

She had been so young.

He didn't know how he'd forgotten that. How he'd failed to factor it in. When he'd been twenty he'd been a bona fide idiot, making an ass of himself at Stanford and enjoying every minute of it. He certainly hadn't been performing for a living, running from this audition to that gig with no guarantee he'd ever make his rent or make some money or even get cast. When Violet had been twenty years old she'd been famously divorcing the much, much older producer who had married her and made her when she'd been only seventeen. No one had called her a mercenary bitch, at least, not to her face. She'd been lauded for her powerful choices and the control she'd taken over her career.

Maybe that was why he'd spent a decade *this furious* with Paige. Because he loved his mother, he truly did, but he'd wanted something else for himself. He'd wanted a girl who wouldn't think of herself first, second, last and always. He'd wanted a girl who would put *him* first. Had he known Paige wouldn't stick with dancing? Had he assumed she would gravitate toward the life she had here in Tuscany, which was more or less arranged around pleasing him?

He'd told her he wanted a partner, but nothing he'd done supported that. Back in Malibu, he'd been jealous of the time she spent practicing and really anything else that took her away from him. This time around he was jealous of her devotion to his own mother. Did he want a partner? Or did he want her to *treat* him like a partner while he did whatever he liked?

Giancarlo didn't much care for the answers that came to him then, in the quiet night, the woman he couldn't seem to get over lying so sweetly beside him. All he knew was that he was tired of fighting this, of holding her at arm's length when he wanted her close. He was tired of the walls he put up. He hated himself more every time he hurt her—

We all must practice what we preach if we are to achieve anything in this life, his father had told him a long time ago as they'd walked the land together, plotting out the placement of vineyards the older man hadn't lived to see to completion. *The trouble is we're all much better at the preaching and not so good at the listening, even to ourselves.*

It had to stop. *He* had to stop. There was no point demanding her trust if he refused to give his own.

He shifted beside her, pulling her close and burying his face in the sweet heat of her neck.

It was time to admit what he'd known for years. She was the only woman he'd ever loved, no matter what she called herself. No matter what she'd done when she was little more than a kid. And he'd never stopped loving her.

"Come sei bella," he whispered into the dark. *How beautiful you are.* And, *"Mi manchi."* *I miss you.* And then, "I love you," in English, though he knew she couldn't hear him.

Giancarlo understood then, in the soft darkness, Paige snuggled close in his arms as if she'd been there all along, that he always had. He always would.

He just needed to tell her when she could hear him.

Paige woke up the next morning in her usual rush when the morning light danced over her face from the skylights above. Giancarlo was next to her, his big body wrapped around her, and she thought, *this is my favorite day.*

She thought that every day, lately. No matter what that voice in her head had to say about it.

And she continued to think it until her stomach went funny in a sudden, hideous lurch, and she had to pull away from him and race for the toilet.

"I must have eaten something strange," she said when she came out of the bathroom to find him frowning with concern, sitting on the side of his bed. She grimaced. "Your mother insisted we eat those weird sausages in Cinque Terre yesterday. One must not have agreed with me."

But Violet wasn't affected. "I have a stomach of steel, my dear girl," she proclaimed when Paige called her to check in, "which is handy when one is living off craft service carts for weeks at a time in all the corners of the earth." And it happened again the next morning. And then the morning after that.

And on the fourth morning, when Paige ran for the bathroom, Giancarlo came in after her and placed a package on the floor beside her as she knelt there, pale and sick and wishing for death. It took her a long moment to calm the wild, lurching beat of her heart. To force back the dizziness as that awful feeling in her stomach retreated again. To feel well enough to focus on what he'd put there in front of her.

Only to feel even more light-headed when she did.

It was a pregnancy test.

"Use it," Giancarlo said, his voice so clipped and stern she didn't dare look up at him to see if his expression matched. She didn't think her stomach could take it. She knew her heart couldn't. "Bring me the result. Then we'll talk."

CHAPTER EIGHT

PAIGE CLIMBED SHAKILY to her feet after his footsteps retreated. She rinsed her mouth out with a scoop of water
from the sink and then she followed the directions on
the package. She waited the requisite amount of time—
she timed it on her phone, to the second—and when the
alarm chirped at her she let herself look.

And just like that, everything was forever altered. But
all she could do was stare at the little stick with its unmistakable plus sign and wish she wasn't naked.

That didn't merely say things about her character, she
thought dimly. It said far more dire things about the kind
of mother she'd be to the tiny little life that was somehow
there inside her—

That was when it hit her. It was a tidal wave of raw
feeling, impossible to categorize or separate or do anything but survive as it all tore through her. Terror. Joy.
Panic. How could she be someone's mother when all
she'd ever known of mothering was Arleen? How could
she be someone's *mother?*

She was holding on to the sink in a death grip when
it passed, tears in her eyes and her knees weak beneath
her. It was hard to breathe, but Paige made herself do it.
In, then out. Deep. Measured.

Then she remembered Giancarlo was waiting for her,

and worse, what he'd said before he'd gone downstairs. And Paige understood then. That this was her worst fear come to life, literally.

That this was the other shoe she'd spent all this time knowing would drop.

She dressed before she went downstairs, glad she'd worn something more substantial than a silly dress the night before. That meant she could truly wrap herself up in her clothes as if they would offer her protection from whatever was about to come. She pulled her hair back into a tight knot at the nape of her neck and she took longer than she should have, and she only went to find him when she understood that dragging this out was going to make it worse. *Was* making it worse.

This will be fine, she told herself as she walked down the wide, smooth stairs, aware that she was delivering herself to her own execution. But there was, despite everything, that teeny tiny sliver of hope deep inside of her that maybe, just maybe, she'd be wrong about this. That he'd surprise her.

We're both adults. These things happen...

Giancarlo waited for her in the open doors that led out to the loggia—which, she supposed with the faintest hint of the hysteria she fought to keep away for fear it might swamp her, was appropriate, given where this baby had likely been conceived. He didn't turn when she came up behind him, he merely held out his hand.

Demonstrating how little he trusted her, she realized, when she finally understood what he was doing and what he expected her to put in his palm. Not her hand, for comfort. The pregnancy test. For proof.

Because he expected tricks and lies from her, even now. Even about this.

She felt something topple over inside of her, some

foundation or other, but she couldn't concentrate on that now. There was only Giancarlo, scowling down at the slender stick in his hand before he bit out a curse and flung it aside.

A thousand smart responses to that moved through her, but she was still shaky from that immense emotional slap that had walloped her upstairs, and she kept them all to herself. He stood there, every muscle tight, even his jaw a hard, granite accusation, and he didn't look at her for a long time.

When he did, it was worse.

Paige waited for him to speak, even as something inside her protested that no, she did not deserve his anger here. That she hadn't done this alone. But she shoved that down, too.

"I thought you were on the pill."

She blinked at the ferocity in his tone. The bite.

"No, you didn't. You used condoms after the first night. Why would you do that if you thought I was on the pill?" He stared at her, and the truth of that rolled over her. For a moment, she couldn't breathe through it. Then she could, and it hurt. It more than hurt. Another foundation turned to dust in an instant. "Oh."

"Tell me," he said in that vicious, cruel way she hadn't heard in almost a month now, so long she'd forgotten how awful it was, how deeply it clawed into her, "what possible reason you could have for sleeping with a man without protection?"

"You did the same thing." But her tongue felt too thick and her head buzzed and she'd known this would happen. Maybe not *this*. Maybe not a pregnancy. But that look on his face. She'd always known she'd see that again. She hadn't understood, until now, how very much she'd wanted to be wrong. "You were right there with me."

154   AT THE COUNT'S BIDDING

"I thought you were on the pill."

She felt helpless. Terrified. Sick. "Why?"

He swore again, not in Italian this time, and she flinched. "What kind of question is that? Because you were before."

"That was different." She was too shaken to think about what she was saying, so she told him the truth without any varnishing. "My mother was terrified I'd end up pregnant at sixteen and forced to raise the baby, like she was with me, so she had me on the pill from the moment I hit puberty."

"And you stopped?" He sounded furious and disbelieving, and Paige didn't understand. How could he think she'd planned this? How could she have, even if she'd wanted to? *You knew he didn't use anything that first night. Why didn't you say something?* But she knew. She hadn't wanted him to stop. She'd wanted him more than anything. "Why the hell would you do something like that?"

"I told you."

Paige was whispering, and she'd backed up so her spine was against the far side of the open doorway as if the house might keep her from collapsing to the floor, but Giancarlo hadn't moved at all. He didn't have to move. His black fury took up all the air. It blocked out the sun.

This is what you deserve, her mother's voice said in her head, filled with a sick glee. *This is what happens to little whores like you, Nicola. You end up like me.*

"You're the only man I've slept with the past ten years," she told him, bald and unflinching. He let out a sound she couldn't interpret and so she kept going, because she was certain she could explain this to him so he would understand. He had to understand. They were going to be parents whether he liked it or not. "You're the only man I've ever slept with, Giancarlo."

"Do not try to sell me that nonsense, not now," he barked at her, as if the words were welling up from somewhere deep inside of him. "I didn't believe the story that you were a virgin then, not even when I thought I could trust you. I'll hand it to you, though. You really do remember all the tortured details of the lies you spin."

"What are you talking about?" Paige shook her head, trying to keep her panic at bay, trying to keep the tears from her voice, and not really succeeding at either. "Who lies about being a virgin at twenty?"

"I can't believe I fell for this twice," he spat, his gaze a molten fury of dark gold, his mouth grim. "I can't believe I walked straight into this. Let me guess. You've never given motherhood a moment's thought, but today, as you gazed upon the test that confirmed your pregnancy, something stirred within you that you'd never felt before." His laugh felt like acid. "Is that about right?"

"Why are you talking to me like I planned this?" she cried. "No one forced you to have sex with me! And no one forced you to do it without a condom!"

"You're good," he said, still in that horrible way that curled inside of her, oily and thick. "I'll give you that. I never saw this coming. I thought I was being too hard on you. I was falling in love with you all over again, but in the end, you're just like her. You always have been. *I'm such an idiot.*"

"For all you know I have no intention of keeping it," she threw at him, desperate to make him look at her like a person again, not like a scam with two legs. Exactly the way he had ten years ago, when he'd waved that magazine in the air outside her apartment and she'd almost wished he'd thrown it at her—because that would be better, she'd thought then, and less violent than that look on his face in that moment before he'd turned and walked away.

But the look of contempt he gave her now was not an improvement.

And his words finally penetrated. *I was falling in love with you.*

"Am I to understand that this is your threat?" he asked in that low, lethal way of his that made her shudder. That made that hollow thing inside of her grow wide and grow teeth. That made it perfectly clear any love he might have felt for her was very much past tense. "I applaud you, *Nicola*," and that name was worse than acid. If he'd hauled off and hit her, he couldn't have hurt her more. "Most women would dance around the issue. But you, as ever, go right to the heart of it."

"I'm not threatening you," she said wildly, only realizing when her cheeks felt cool in the breeze that tears were running down her face. "This wasn't planned. I don't know why you insist on thinking the worst of me—"

"Stop." It was a command, harsh and cold. "I'm not doing this with you again. I'm not pretending it matters what you say. You'll do what you like, *Nicola.* You always do. And like a cockroach I have no doubt you'll survive whatever happens and come back even stronger. Violet's protégé in more ways than I realized."

"Why would I force a child on you?" she demanded. "Why?"

"Perhaps you thought your payday last time wasn't enough," he bit out. "Perhaps you want to make certain you really will make it into Violet's will. Perhaps you're looking forward to selling as many tabloid stories as you can. It wouldn't take much effort to position yourself as one of those celebrities for no apparent reason, not with

Violet's grandchild in your clutches. To say nothing of the Alessi estate. You must know by now I'd never keep my heritage from my own child." He was nearly white with fury. "Which are only a few of the reasons I never wanted one."

"Giancarlo—"

But he straightened, his expression changed, and it was as if he disappeared, right there in front of her. As if the man she knew was simply…gone.

"If you decide to have the baby, inform my lawyers," he told her with a hideous finality that shuddered through her like an earthquake. There was none of that bright gold fury in his eyes any longer when he looked at her. There was only emptiness. A dark, cold nothing that made everything inside her twist into blackness. "I will pay whatever child support you deem necessary, and I will pay more if you honor my wish for privacy and keep my name to yourself. But I don't expect that's in your nature, is it? How can you leverage my privacy to your best advantage?"

"Please," she said, pleading with him now, unable to stop the sobs that poured out of her, worse, perhaps, because she'd always known this was coming. But not today. Not like this. She still wasn't ready. "You can't—"

"Do not attempt to contact my mother again." His voice got dangerous then. Flint and fury, and still, he was a stranger. "I will have you arrested and thrown in jail and no judge in any country would ever grant a woman with mental problems and a prison record custody of a child over me. I want you to remember that. You so much as text Violet and you'll never see that child again."

"Stop," she threw at him, in a terrible whisper. "You can't think—"

"A driver will pick you up in an hour," he told her, and

he was merciless. Pitiless. As if he was made of marble and was that soft, that bendable. "I want you gone. And I never, ever want to see you again. Not in ten minutes. Not in another ten years. Is that clear?"

Paige couldn't reply. She was shaking so hard she was afraid she'd fall over, the tears were hot and endless, and he looked at her as if she was a stranger. As if he was. Crafted of marble, but far crueler. Marble might crush her. But he'd torn her into pieces first.

"Do you understand?" he asked, even harsher than before.

"Yes," Paige managed to say. "I understand." She scrubbed her hands over her face and sucked in a breath and tried one last time. "Giancarlo—"

But he was already gone.

It was over.

The slippery December roads were treacherous but the wind outside was even worse, rattling his SUV and shaking the skeletons of the trees on either side of the New England country roads.

And inside him, Giancarlo knew, it was colder and darker still.

He had not been in a good mood to begin with when he'd left Logan International Airport in Boston more than two hours earlier on this latest quest to find Paige. It was fair to say he'd been in a black mood for the past three months.

The tiny, lonely little Maine town a hundred miles from anywhere sat under a fresh coat of snow, lights twinkling as the December evening fell sudden and fast in the middle of what other places might still consider the afternoon, and he felt the stirrings of adrenaline as he navigated through the very few streets that comprised the village to the small, white clapboard house that was his destination.

He'd hired detectives. He'd scoured half of the West Coast and a good part of the East Coast himself. This was the last place on earth he'd have thought to look for her—which was, he could admit, why it had no doubt made such a perfect hiding place.

This time, he knew she was here. He'd seen the photo on his mobile when he'd landed in Boston from Italy, taken this very morning. But he wouldn't believe it until he saw her with his own eyes.

He could admit the place held a certain desolate charm, Giancarlo thought grimly as he climbed from the car, the boots he only ever wore at ski resorts in places like Vail or St. Moritz crunching into the snow beneath him. The drive from Boston into the remote state of Maine had reminded him of the books he'd had to read while in his American high school. Lonely barns in barren fields and the low winter sky pressing down, gray and sullen. Here and there a hint of the wild, rocky Atlantic coast, lighthouses the only bit of faint cheer against the coming dark.

It felt like living inside his own bleak soul, in the great mess he'd made.

Giancarlo navigated his way over the salted sidewalk and up the old front steps to the clapboard house's front door, able to hear the faint sound of piano music from inside. DANCE LESSONS, read the sign on the door, making his chest feel tight.

He stopped there, frozen on the porch with his hand on the doorknob, because he heard her voice. For the first time since that last, ugly morning in his Tuscan cottage. Counting off the beat.

Wedging its way into his heart like one of the vicious icicles that hung from the roof above him.

He wrenched the door open and walked inside, and then she was right there in front of him after all this time. *Right there.*

She took his breath away.

Giancarlo's heart thundered in his chest and he forced himself to take stock of his surroundings. The ground floor of this house was its dance studio, an open space with only a few pillars and a class in session. And the woman he'd accused of a thousand different scams was not lounging about being fed bonbons she'd bought with his mother's money or her own infamy, she was teaching the class. To what looked like a pack of very pink-faced, very uncoordinated young girls.

He was standing in what passed for the small studio's lobby and if the glares from the women sitting in the couches and chairs along the wall were anything to go by, he'd disrupted the class with his loud entrance.

Not that Giancarlo cared about them in the slightest.

Paige, he noted as he forced himself to breathe again and not do anything rash, did not look at him at all, which was a feat indeed, given the mirrors on every available wall. She merely carried on teaching as if he was nothing to her.

But he refused to accept that. Particularly if it were true.

The class continued. And Giancarlo studied her as she moved in front of the small collection of preadolescents, calling out instructions and corrections and encouragement in equal measure. She looked as if she hadn't slept much, but only when he studied her closely. Her hair was still that inky black, darker now than he remembered, and he wondered if it was the sun that brought out its auburn hints. She moved the way she did in all his dreams, all of that grace and ease, as if she flowed rather than walked.

And she was still slim, with only the faintest thickening at her belly to tell him what he hadn't known until now, what he'd been afraid to wonder about until he'd finally tracked her down in what had to be, literally, one of the farthest places she could go in the opposite direction of Bel Air. And him.

That she was keeping the baby. *His* baby.

Giancarlo didn't know what that was inside of him then. Relief. Fury. A new surge of determination. All the rest of the dark things he'd always felt for this woman, turned inside out. All mixed together until it felt new. Until he did.

She was keeping their baby.

He would have loved her anyway. He did. But he couldn't help but view her continuing pregnancy as a sign. As hope.

As far more than he deserved.

It seemed like twenty lifetimes before the class ended, and the women in the chairs collected their young. He paid them no attention as they herded their charges past him out into the already-pitch-black night; he simply waited, arms crossed and his brooding gaze on Paige.

And eventually, the last stranger left and slammed the door shut behind her small town curiosity, and it was only the two of them in the glossy, bright room. Paige and him and all their history, and she still didn't look at him.

"You decided to keep it." He didn't know why he said it like that, fierce and low, and he watched her stiffen, but it was too late to call it back.

"If you came here for an apology," she said in a low voice he hardly recognized, and then she turned to face him fully and he blinked because she hardly looked like herself, "you can shove it right up your—"

"I don't want an apology." It was temper, he realized belatedly. Pure fury that transformed her lovely face and turned her eyes nearly gray. As if she would kill him with her own hands if she crossed the wide, battered floor and got too close to him, and there was no reason that should shock him and intrigue him in equal measure. "I spent three months tracking you down, Paige."

Her eyes narrowed and if anything, grew darker.

"Are you sure that's what you want to call me?" she threw at him. "I know that historically you've had some trouble keeping my name straight."

Giancarlo felt a muscle move in his cheek and realized he was clenching his jaw.

"I know your name."

"I can't tell you how that delights me." Her temper was like a fog in the air between them, thick and impenetrable, and he thought she might even have growled at him. "The only thing that would delight me more would be if you'd turn around and go away and pretend we never met. That's what I've been doing and so far? It's been the best three months of my life."

He had that coming. He knew that. He told himself it didn't even sting.

"I understand," he began as carefully as he could, "that—"

"Don't bother," she snapped, cutting him off. He couldn't recall she'd ever done that before. In fact, there was only one person in the world who interrupted him with impunity and she'd given birth to him—and wasn't terribly thrilled with him at the moment, either. "I don't want your explanations. I don't care."

She turned away from him, but the mirrors betrayed her, showing him a hint of the Paige he knew in the way her face twisted before she wrestled it back under control. Another sliver of hope, if he was a desperate man. He was.

Giancarlo walked farther into the studio, still studying her. She was in bare feet and a pair of leggings, with a loose tunic over them that drooped down over one shoulder. She was the most beautiful thing he'd ever seen. He wanted to press his mouth to the bare skin of her shoulder, then explore that brand-new belly of hers. Then, perhaps, that molten heat of hers that he knew had only ever been his. He was primitive enough to relish that.

He'd believed her. It had taken him longer than it should have to admit that to himself. He'd believed her then, and he believed her now—but the fact she'd only ever given herself to him had meanings he'd been afraid to explore. He wasn't afraid anymore.

Giancarlo had lost her once. What was there to fear now? He'd already lived through the worst thing that could happen to him. Twice.

"How did you find this place?" he asked as he walked toward her. He meant, *how did you settle on this small, faraway, practically hidden town it took me three months to find?* "Why did you come here in the first place?"

"I can't imagine why you care." Paige shoved her things into a bag and then straightened. "I doubt that you do." She scowled at him when he kept coming, when he only stopped when he was within touching distance. "What do you want, Giancarlo?"

"I don't know." That wasn't true, but he didn't know how to express the rest of it, and not when she kept throwing him like this. He realized he'd never seen her angry before. Or anything but wild—wildly in love, wildly apologetic, wild beneath his hands. Never cold like this. Never furious. He supposed he deserved that, too. "You're so angry."

Paige actually laughed then, and it wasn't her real laugh. It was a bitter little thing that made his chest hurt.

More than it already did, than it had since that morning in Tuscany.

"You're unbelievable," she whispered. Then she shook her head. "I could be angry about any number of things, Giancarlo, but let's pick one at random, shall we? You told me you never wanted to see me again, and I happen to think that's the best plan you've had yet. So please, go back to wherever you came from. Go back to Italy and ruin someone else's life. Leave me—leave *us*—alone."

He wanted to pull her close to him. He wanted to taste her. He *wanted*. But he settled for shaking his head slightly and watching her face, instead, as if she might disappear again if he took his eyes off her.

"I'm sorry," he said into the tense quiet. "It's not that I'm not listening to you. But I've never seen you angry, ever. I didn't think it was something you knew how to do."

Paige blinked, and pulled the bag higher on her shoulder, gripping the strap with both of her hands.

"It wasn't," she said simply. "Especially around you. But it turns out, that's not a very healthy way to live a life. It ends up putting you at the mercy of terrible people because you never say no. You never tell them to stop. You never stand up for yourself until it's too late."

And when her eyes met his, they slammed into him so hard it was like a punch, and Giancarlo understood she meant him. That *he* had done those things to her. That he was one more terrible person to her. It tasted sour in his mouth, that realization. And he hated it with almost as much force as he understood, at last, that it was true. That he'd treated her horribly. That he was precisely the kind of man he'd been raised to detest. That was why he'd come after her, was it not? To face these things.

But that didn't make hearing it any easier.

"That is not the kind of life my baby is going to live, Giancarlo," Paige told him fiercely. "Not if I have anything to say about it." She tilted her chin up as if she expected him to argue. "This baby will have a *home.* This baby will be *wanted.* Loved. Celebrated. This baby is not a mistake. Or a problem. This baby will *belong* somewhere. *With me.*"

As if she really had punched him, and hard, it took Giancarlo a moment to recover from all her fierceness, and more, what it told him. And when he did, it was to see her storming across the room.

Away from him. Again.

"Come have dinner with me," he began.

"No."

"Coffee then." He eyed her, remembering that tiny bump. "Or whatever you can drink."

"And again, no."

"Paige." He didn't have any idea what he was doing and he thought he hated that almost as much as the distance between them, which seemed much, much worse now that they were standing in the same room. "It's my baby, too."

She whirled back around, so fast he thought someone without her grace might have toppled over, and then she jabbed a finger in the air in a manner he imagined was meant to show him how very much she wished it was something sharp she could stick in a far more tender area.

"She is *my* baby!" And her voice grew louder with each word. "Mine. I knew I was pregnant with the baby of a man who *hated me* for *five whole minutes* before you ripped me into shreds and walked away, but believe me, Giancarlo, I heard you. You want nothing to do with me. You want nothing to do with this baby. And that is *fine*—"

"I never said I wanted nothing to do with the baby," he protested. "Quite the opposite."

"We can debate that when there's a baby, then," she hurled at him, hardly stopping to take a breath. "Which by my calculations gives me six months and then some of freedom from having to talk to you."

"But I want to talk to you." And he didn't care that he sounded more demanding than apologetic, then. She might truly want nothing to do with him, ever again, and he understood he deserved that. But he had to be sure. "I want to see how you're doing. I want to understand what happened between us in Italy."

"No, you don't."

And her face twisted again, but her eyes were still that dark gray and they still burned, and he couldn't tell what she wanted. Only that as ever, he was hurting her. The way he always did.

"You don't want to understand *me*," Paige told him. "You want me to understand *you*. And believe me, I already do. I understood you when you were the very wealthy, semifamous director who took an unexpected interest in a backup dancer. I understood you when you were the noble son standing up for his mother against the potential lunatic who had infiltrated her home behind your back. I even understood you when you were the beleaguered, betrayed ex, drawn back into an intense sexual relationship against his better judgment by the deceitful little seductress he couldn't put behind him. I *understood* myself sick."

She pulled in a breath, as if it hurt her, which was when Giancarlo realized he hadn't breathed throughout this. That he couldn't seem to draw a breath at all.

"And then," Paige continued, her voice strong and even, "once I left, I understood that you have never, ever pretended to be there for me in any way. Not ten years ago. Not now. It never crossed your mind to *ask me* why I did something like sell those pictures, just as it never occurred to you to ask me how *I* felt about finding myself pregnant. The only thing you care about is you."

"Paige."

She ignored him. "You never asked me anything at all. You've never treated me liked anything but a storm you had to weather." She shook her head. "You're the damned hurricane, Giancarlo, but you blame me for the rain." She shifted then, her hands moving to shelter that little bump, as if she needed to protect it from him, and he thought that might be the worst cut, the deepest wound. He was surprised to find he still stood. "All I want from you is what you've always given me. Your absence."

The room seemed dizzy with her words when she'd stopped speaking, as if the mirrors could hardly bear the weight of them. Or maybe that was him. Maybe he'd fallen down and he simply couldn't tell the difference.

"You said *she.*"

"What?"

Giancarlo didn't know where that had come from. He hadn't known he meant to speak at all. He was too busy seeing himself through her eyes—and not liking it at all. "Before. You called the baby a *she.*"

"Yes." She seemed worn-out then, in a sudden rush. As if she'd lanced a wound with a surge of adrenaline and the poison had all run out, leaving nothing behind it. "I'm having a little girl in May."

"A daughter." His voice was gentle, yet filled with something it took him a moment to identify. *Wonder.* He heard it move through the room and he saw her shudder as she pulled in a breath, and he knew, somehow, that everything wasn't lost. Not yet. Not quite yet. "We're having a daughter."

"Go away, Giancarlo," she said, but it was a whisper. Just a whisper with none of that fury behind it, and a hint of the kind of sadness he'd become all too familiar with these past few months. And he wanted nothing more than to protect her, even if it was from himself.

Perhaps especially then.

"I can do that," he said gruffly. "Tonight. But I'll keep coming back, Paige. Every day until you talk to me. I can be remarkably persuasive."

"Is that a threat?" She rubbed a hand over the back of her neck, and he thought she looked tired again, but not threatened. "This isn't your land in Italy. I'm not a prisoner here."

"I don't want to keep you prisoner," he said, which was not entirely true. He reminded himself he was a civilized man. Or the son of one anyway, little as he might have lived up to his father's standards lately. "I want to have dinner with you."

She eyed him, and he could see the uncertainty on her pretty face. "That's all?"

"Do you want me to lie to you?" he asked quietly. "It's a start. Just give me a start."

She shook her head, but her eyes seemed less gray now and more that changeable blue-green he recognized, and Giancarlo couldn't help but consider that progress.

"What if I don't want a start?" she asked after a moment. "Any start? We've had two separate starts marked by ten years of agony and now this. It's not fun."

He smiled. "Then it's dinner. Everyone needs to eat dinner. Especially pregnant women, I understand."

"But not with you," Paige said, and there was something different in her voice then. Some kind of resolve. "Not again. It's not worth it."

She turned away again and headed toward the door he could see in the back, and this time, he could tell, she was really going to leave.

And Giancarlo knew he should let her go. He knew he'd done more than enough already. The practical side of him pointed out that six months was a reasonable amount of time to win a person over, to say nothing of the following lifetime of the child they'd made. *Their daughter.* He had all the time in the world.

He'd spent three months trying to find her—what was another night? He knew he should forfeit this battle, the better to win the war. But he couldn't do it.

Giancarlo couldn't watch her walk away again.

CHAPTER NINE

LATER, PAIGE THOUGHT, she would hate herself for how difficult it was to march across the studio floor toward the door, her car beyond, and the brand-new life she was in the middle of crafting.

Later, she would despair of the kind of person she must be, that her heart had somersaulted nearly out of her chest when Giancarlo had stormed in, startling her so profoundly it had taken her a long moment to remember why that instant sense of relief she'd felt was more than a little sick. Later, she would beat herself up about how little she wanted to walk away from him, even now.

But first she had to really do it. Walk away. Mean what she said. Leave him standing—

Her first clue that he'd moved at all was a rush of air over her shoulder and then his hands were on her, gentle and implacable at once. He turned her, lifted her, and in a single smooth shift she was in his arms. Held high against his chest, so she was surrounded. By his scent. By his strength.

A scant breath away from that cruel mouth, that sensual mouth.

Much too close to everything she wanted, so desperately, to forget.

"Put me down."

Her voice was so quiet it was hardly a breath of sound—but she knew, somehow, what that dark gold fury in his gaze was now. It was a warning that this situation could get out of control quickly, with a single kiss, and Paige rather doubted she'd be able to maintain any kind of moral high ground if she let him deep inside her again.

Especially because she wanted him there. Even now.

"First of all," Giancarlo said, in that low and lethal way that still moved over her like a seduction, making her very bones feel weak, "I do not hate you. I have never hated you. I have spent years trying to convince myself that I hated you only to fail miserably at it, again and again."

"Then you only *act* as if you hate me," she grated at him, refusing to put her arm over his shoulders, holding herself tight and unyielding against him as if that might save her. From herself. "That's much better."

He stopped next to the line of old armchairs and love seats that sat against the wall and set her down in the biggest one, then shocked her to the core by kneeling down in front of her. She froze, which was why it took her a moment to notice that he'd caged her in, his hands gripping the back of the chair behind her, putting his face about as close as it could get to hers without actually touching her.

"Why did you sell those photographs?" he asked. Quietly, his dark gaze trained on her face. So there was no chance at all he didn't see the heat that flashed over her, making her cheeks warm.

"What can that possibly matter now?"

"I think you're right about a lot of things," he said, sounding somewhere between grim and determined. And something else she wasn't sure she'd ever heard before. "But especially this. I should have asked. I'm asking now."

And the trouble was, she loved him. She'd always loved him. And she'd waited a decade for him to ask. If he'd asked in Italy, she might have sugarcoated it, but things were different now. *She* was different now.

She owed it to the life inside of her to be the kind of woman she wanted her daughter to become. That strong. That unafraid. That unflinching when necessary.

"My mother was a drunk," Paige said flatly. "Her dreams of riches and fame and escape from our awful little hometown came to a screeching halt when she got pregnant with me in high school, so it worked out well that I could dance. The minute I was done with high school she took me to Los Angeles. She made me use my middle name as a stage name because she thought it was fancy, and everyone knew you had to be fancy to be famous. She decided she made an excellent stage mother, if your definition of a stage mother is that she took all the money and then yelled at me to get out there and make more."

"That is the common Hollywood definition, yes," Giancarlo said drily, but she couldn't stop now. Not even to laugh.

"A drunk Arleen was one thing," Paige told him. "But a little while before I met you, my mother met a meth dealer. His name was Denny, and let me tell you, he was *so* nice to us. A new best friend." Her mouth twisted. "A month later, she was thousands of dollars in the hole and he was a little less friendly. Two months later, she was hundreds of thousands of dollars in debt to him, there was no possible way she could get out of it and he stopped pretending. He laid it out for me." She met Giancarlo's gaze and held it. *Unflinching,* she told herself. No matter that she'd never wanted him to know the kind of dirt that clung to her. Not when his whole life was so clean, so pretty, so bathed in light. "I could work it off on my back, or I could watch him kill her. Or—and this was an afterthought—I could make some money off my rich new boyfriend instead."

"Paige." He breathed her name as if it was one of his Italian curses, or perhaps a prayer, and she didn't know when he'd dropped his hands down to take hers, only that his hands were so warm, so strong, and she was far weaker than she wanted to be if he was what made her feel strong. Wasn't she? "Why didn't you tell me this? Why didn't you let me help you?"

"Because I was ashamed," she said, and her voice cracked, but she didn't look away from him. "Your mother was *Violet Sutherlin.* My mother was a drug addict who sold herself when she ran out of money, and it still wasn't enough. Who wanted to sell *me* because until I met you, I was a virgin."

He paled slightly, and she felt his hands tighten around hers, and she pushed on.

"The first night I spent with you, she realized I'd slept with you," Paige said, aware that she sounded hollow, when still, she couldn't regret it. Not a moment of that long, perfect night. Not even knowing what came after. "And when I got home that next day, she slapped me so hard it actually made my ears ring. But not enough to block her out. I'd already ruined her life by being born, you see. The least I could have done was let her sell the one commodity she had—I mean my virginity—to the highest bidder. She'd had the whole thing planned out with some friends of Denny's."

"How did I miss this?" Giancarlo asked, his voice a hoarse scrape in the empty studio.

"Because I wanted you to miss it." Her voice was fierce. "Because you were my single rebellion. My escape. The only thing I'd ever had that was good. And all mine. And you came without any strings." She dropped her gaze then, to where their hands were clasped tight. "But she was my mother."

He muttered something in Italian.

"I think," Paige said, because she had to finish now, "that if I hadn't met you, even if I'd had a different boyfriend, I would have just slept with whoever Denny told me to sleep with. It would have been easier."

"It would have been prostitution," Giancarlo said, viciously, but she knew that this time, it wasn't directed at her.

"What difference would it have made?" she asked, and she meant that. She shrugged. "I didn't know anything else. A lot of the dancers slept around and let the men help with their rent. They didn't call it prostitution—they called it dating. With benefits. Maybe I wouldn't have minded it, if I'd started there. But I'd met you." She blew out a breath and met his dark gold gaze. "And I was twenty years old. My mother told me a thousand times a day that men like you had a million girls like me. That I'd thrown myself away on you, that you would get sick of me sooner rather than later and we'd have nothing to show for it. And she, by God, wanted something to show for all her suffering."

"How, pray, had *she* suffered?" His tone was icy, and it warmed something inside of her. As if maybe all those foundations she'd thought he'd shattered in Italy had only frozen and were coming back now as they warmed. As she did.

"It wasn't my idea," Paige said quietly, because this was the important part. "Denny insisted that sex sold.

That you were worth an outrageous amount of money. And I thought—I really thought—that I owed her something. That it was just what love looked like. Because I might have ruined her life, but she was my mother. I loved her. I owed her."

"You don't have to tell me any more," Giancarlo said, his voice a deep rumble. "I understand."

"I loved you, too," Paige whispered. "But I'd had twenty years of Arleen and only a couple months of you. I thought she was the real thing and you were just a dream. I thought if it was really a true thing between you and me, you'd try to understand why I did it. But I wasn't surprised when you didn't."

He let out a breath, as if he'd suffered a blow.

"I'm so sorry," he said quietly. So quietly she almost didn't notice the way it sneaked into her, adding fuel to that small fire that still burned for him, for them. That always would. "I wish you'd come to me. I wish I'd seen what was happening beneath my nose. I wish I'd had any idea what you were going through."

"It doesn't matter now." And she found she meant that. She kept going, because she needed to finish. To see it through. "I did it. I got half a million dollars for those pictures and I lost you. I gave the money to my mother. It was enough to pay Denny and then some. I was such an idiot—I thought that meant we'd be fine."

"How long?" he asked, and she knew what he meant.

"Another month or so and the money was gone. Then she was in debt again. And it turned out Denny was even less understanding than he'd been before, because there was no rich boyfriend any longer. There was only me. And he was pretty clear about the one thing I was good at. How could I argue? The entire world had seen me in action. I was a commodity again."

"My God."

"I don't know about God," Paige said. "It was the LAPD who busted Denny on something serious enough to put him away for fifteen years. My mother lost her supplier, which meant she lost her mind. The last time I saw her, she was on the streets and she might be there still. She might not have made it this long. I don't know." She lifted her chin to look him in the eye. "And that's what happened ten years ago."

"You can't possibly feel guilty about that." He sounded incredulous. He frowned at her. "Paige. Please. You did everything you possibly could for that woman. Literally. You can't stop people when they want to destroy themselves—you can only stop them from taking you along with them."

She shrugged again, as if that might shift the constriction in her throat. "She's still my mother. I still love…if not her, then who she was supposed to be."

Giancarlo looked at her for a long time. So long she forgot she'd been too ashamed to tell him this. So long she lost herself again, the way she always did, in that face of his, those dark eyes, that mouth.

"I'm so sorry," he said, his voice so low it seemed to move inside of her, like heat. "I wouldn't blame you if you hated me. I don't think I understand why you don't."

"Because my whole life, Giancarlo," she whispered, unable to hide anything from him, not after all this time and all the ways they'd hurt each other, not any longer, "you're the only person I've ever loved. The only one who loved me back."

He shifted back and then he reached over to brush moisture from beneath her eyes, and Paige reminded herself that she was supposed to be resisting him. Fighting him off. Standing up for herself. She couldn't understand how she could feel as if she was doing that when, clearly, she was doing the opposite.

"Violet adores you," he said then. "And despite her excursions around the Tuscan countryside purely to be recognized and adored, she does not, in fact, like more than a handful of people. She trusts far fewer."

Paige made a face. "She has no idea who I really am."

He smiled then. "Of course she does. She tells me she's known exactly who you are from the moment she met you. Why else would she let you so deep into the family?"

But Paige shook her head at that, confused. And something more than simply confused.

"Why would she do that?" she whispered.

"Because my father was a good man," Giancarlo said, his hands hard and warm and tight on hers again, "and a kind man, but a cold one. And shortly after I told her you'd left she informed me that the only time in my life when I didn't act just like him, inaccessible and aloof and insufferable—her words—" and his mouth crooked then "—was when I was with you. Ten years and three months ago."

"She knew," Paige whispered, trying to take it in. "Is that why she was so kind to me?"

"That," Giancarlo said, a certain urgency in his voice that made her shift against the chair and tell herself it was only nerves, "and the fact that no matter what you might have been taught, it is not that difficult to be kind to you."

"You've found it incredibly difficult," she pointed out, and it was getting harder by the moment to control the things shaking inside her, the things shaking loose. "Impossible, even."

"I am a selfish, arrogant ass," he said, so seriously that she laughed out loud.

"Well," she said when the laughter faded. "That's not the word I would have used. But if the shoe fits…"

"I am my mother's son," he said simply. "I was born wealthy and aristocratic and, apparently, deeply sorry for myself. It took me all of an hour to realize I'd been completely out of line that day in Italy, Paige. It wasn't about you. It was about my own childhood, about the vows I'd made that only you have ever tempted me to break—but I have no excuse." He shook his head, his mouth thinning. "I know you didn't try to trick me. I considered chasing you down at the airfield and dragging you back with me, but I thought you needed space from the madman who'd said those things to you. I took the earliest flight I could the following day, but when I got to Los Angeles, you weren't there. Your things were packed up and shipped out to storage, but you never went there in person."

"That storage facility is in Bakersfield," she said, blinking. "Did you go there?"

"I haunted it," he said, his gaze dark and steady on hers. "For weeks."

There was no denying the heat that swirled in her then, too much like hope, like light, when she knew better than to—

But he was here. He was kneeling down in front of her even after she'd told him the kind of person she'd been at twenty. The kind of life she'd have led, if not for him. The kind of world she'd been raised in. He was *trying,* clearly.

And Paige didn't want to be right. She wanted to be happy. Just once, she wanted to be *happy.*

"I was going to ship it wherever I settled," she told him, letting that revolutionary thought settle into her bones. "There was no point carting it all around with me when I didn't know where I was going."

"What 'all' are you talking about?" he asked, his tone

dry. "It is perhaps three boxes, I am informed, after brib-ing the unscrupulous owner of that facility a shockingly small amount of money to see for myself." His expres-sion dared her to protest that, but she didn't. If anything, she had to bite back a smile. "My mother requires more baggage for a long afternoon in Santa Monica."

Paige shook her head, realizing she was drinking in his nearness instead of standing up for herself and the little life inside of her. That she owed both of them more than that. That the fact she felt lighter than she had in years was nice, but it didn't change anything. That wasn't happiness, that was chemistry, and she'd already seen where that led, hadn't she? She needed more.

Paige might not be certain what *she* deserved, but her daughter deserved everything. *Everything.* She would use Arleen as her base and do the exact opposite. That meant many things, among them, not settling for a man—even if it was Giancarlo Alessi—simply because he was in front of her. Paige had watched that dynamic in action again and again and again. Her baby would not.

"How did you find me?" she asked, keeping all of her brand-new hopes, all of her wishes and all of her real-izations out of her voice. Or she tried. "And more im-portantly, why?"

"The how is simple. I remembered you said you wanted to see the fall leaves change color in Vermont."

"I did?"

"When we first met. It was autumn in Los Angeles, hot and bright, and you told me you wanted to see real seasons. You also said you wanted to live near the sea and see the snow." He shrugged. "I decided that all those things pointed to New England. After that, I utilized the fact that I am a very wealthy, very motivated, very de-termined man to hunt you down."

"Giancarlo—"

"And the why is this." He reached into his pocket and pulled out a small box, and smiled slightly when she jerked back.

"No." It was automatic. And loud.

Giancarlo didn't seem at all fazed.

"This was my grandmother's diamond," he said. He cracked open the box and held it out, and she remembered, then, that first night with him in Italy, when he'd stood with his hand out and she'd thought he could stand like that forever, if he had to. His dark gaze met hers, and held. "I had the ring made for you ten years ago."

Paige felt her eyes flood then, and she let them, covering her mouth with her hands, unable to speak. So he did.

"Everything you said about me is true," he told her. "I can't deny any of it. But I want to understand you, Paige. I want to dedicate the next ten years to learning every single thing that makes you *you*. I don't simply want a partner, I want to be one. I want to be yours. I want you to yell at me and put me in my place and I want to help you teach our daughter never to surrender herself to terrible men like her father." His voice was scratchy then. "Not ever."

"Stop," she said, and she didn't mean to reach over to him. She didn't mean to slide her hand along his perfect, lean cheek. "I never gave you anything I didn't want to give. You must know that. It was only that I knew it would end."

"This won't," he whispered. "It hasn't in ten years. It won't in ten more, or ten after that, or ever." He leaned forward, sliding his hand over her belly to cup that small, unmistakable swell, and the smile that moved over that mouth of his broke her heart and made it leap at once. Then he made it far worse, leaning in to press a reverent kiss there. "I love you, Paige. Please. Let me show you."

"I love you, too," she whispered, because what was the point in pretending otherwise? They'd already lost so much time. "But trust is a whole lot more than a pretty ring. I'll always be the woman who sold you out."

"And I'll always be the man who greeted the news of his daughter's impending arrival like a pig," he retorted. "Based on the wild fears of the four-year-old boy I haven't been in decades."

"That sounds like a recipe for disaster."

"I know." He shifted then, pulling the ring from its box and slipping it onto her finger. It fit perfectly, and Paige couldn't seem to breathe. And his eyes were so bright, and she felt three times the size of her skin, and she didn't want to let him go this time. She didn't want to sacrifice him, ever again. "Believe me, I know, but it's not. It only means we've tested each other and we're still here."

He picked up her hand with its sparkling diamond and carried it to his lips. "Wear this and we'll work on it," he murmured, his eyes on her and the words seeming to thud straight into her heart, her flesh, her bones. "Every day. I promise I won't rest until you're happy enough to burst."

"Until we both are," she corrected him.

And then he leaned in close, and he wrapped himself around her and he kissed her. Again and again. Until she was dizzy with longing and love. Until neither one of them could breathe.

And Giancarlo gave her a detailed demonstration of his commitment to the cause, right there on one of the sofas in that bright, big room.

CHAPTER TEN

SHE MADE HIM work for it. And she made him wait.

And Giancarlo had no one to blame but himself for either.

"How do I know that you want to marry me and not simply to claim the baby in some appalling display of machismo?" she had asked him that first night, naked and astride him, when his intentions toward her, personally, could not have been more obvious.

"Set me any test," he'd told her then. "I'll pass it."

She'd considered him for a long moment, her inky hair in that tangle he loved and her eyes that brilliant green. And the way she fit him. *God, the fit.*

"Don't ask me again," she said, her tone very serious, her green gaze alight. "I'll let you know when I'm ready."

"Take your time," he'd told her with all the patience of a desperate man. "I want you to trust me."

"I want to trust you, too," she'd whispered in return.

But the truth was they learned to trust each other.

He flew back and forth from Italy as needed, and didn't argue when sometimes, she refused to go with him. He shared her tiny studio apartment with her in her snowy New England town, a hundred miles or more from anywhere, and he didn't complain. He shoveled snow. He salted paths. He made certain her car was well-maintained and he never pressured her to move.

She told him more about her childhood with that terrible woman. He told her about his childhood with a woman less terrible perhaps, but deeply complicated all the same. And they held each other. They soothed each other.

They came to know each other in all the ways they hadn't had time to get to know each other ten years ago. Layer on top of layer.

Until he came back from another trip to Italy one snowy March weekend and Paige said that maybe, if he had a better place in mind for them to live, she'd consider it.

"I don't know anything about homes," she told him, her attention perhaps *too* focused on the book she held in her lap. "But you seem to have quite a few."

"You make every house I have a home, *il mio amore*," he told her. "Without you, they are but adventures in architecture."

And he had them back in his house in Malibu by the following afternoon, as if they'd never left it ten years ago. The sea in front of him, the mountains behind him and his woman at his side.

Giancarlo had never been happier. Except for one small thing.

"Why haven't you married her yet?" Violet demanded every time she saw him, particularly when Paige was with him. He could only raise his brows at this woman he loved more than he'd imagined it was possible to love anyone, and wait for her to answer.

Which she was happy to do.

"I'm not sure I'll have him, Violet," Paige would reply airily. She would pat her ever-larger belly and smile blandly, and Giancarlo thought that they'd both transitioned from a working relationship to family rather easily. Almost as if Violet had planned it. "I'm considering all my options."

"I don't blame you," Violet would say with a sniff. "He was horrible. I'd tell you he gets that sort of inexcusable behavior from his father but, alas, Count Alessi was the most polite and well-mannered man I ever met. It's all me."

"I don't think anyone thought otherwise," Giancarlo would say then, and everyone would laugh.

But he never asked Paige again. He kept his promise.

"And if a single photograph or unauthorized mention of my daughter appears anywhere, for any reason, in a manner which benefits you without my express, written consent," he told the great screen legend Violet Sutherlin one pretty afternoon, in her office in front of her new assistant so there could be no mistake that he meant business, "you will never see her again. Until she is at least thirty. Do you understand me, Mother? I am no longer that four-year-old. My daughter never will be."

Violet had gazed at him for a long time. She hadn't showed him that smile of hers. She hadn't said anything witty. In the end, she'd only nodded, once. Sharp and jerky.

But he knew she understood that he'd meant it.

Five months and three weeks after the night he'd turned up in Maine, when Paige was big and round and had to walk in a kind of waddle to get down the makeshift aisle, she married him at last in a tiny ceremony on Violet's terrace. Violet presided. The bride and the officiant wept.

Giancarlo smiled with the greatest satisfaction he'd known in his life. And kissed his bride. *His wife.*

"Don't ever torture me like that again," he growled

against her lips when they were in the car and headed home, finally married, the way they should have been more than ten years before.

"Surely you knew I'd marry you," Paige said, laughing. "I've been pretty open about how much I love you."

"I'm not at all certain I deserve you," he said, and was startled when that made great tears well up in her lovely changeable eyes, then roll down her cheeks. "But I've taken that on as a lifelong project."

She smiled at him, the whole world in that smile, the way it had been that long ago day on that set when they'd locked eyes for the first time. And Giancarlo knew without the slightest shred of doubt that this was merely a particularly good day on the long road toward forever. And that they'd walk the whole of it together, just like this.

And then her expression altered, and she grabbed his arm.

"We're going to have a lot of lifelong projects," Paige said, sounding fierce and awed at once. His beautiful wife. "I think my water just broke."

They named their daughter Violetta Grace, after her famous grandmother, who'd insisted, and the less famous one, who'd died before Paige was born and Arleen had gone completely off the rails, and she was perfect.

Extraordinary.

Theirs.

And they spent the rest of their lives teaching her, in a thousand little ways and few great big ones, what it meant to be as happy as they were the moment they met her.

* * * * *

MILLS & BOON®
Hardback – March 2015

ROMANCE

The Taming of Xander Sterne	Carole Mortimer
In the Brazilian's Debt	Susan Stephens
At the Count's Bidding	Caitlin Crews
The Sheikh's Sinful Seduction	Dani Collins
The Real Romero	Cathy Williams
His Defiant Desert Queen	Jane Porter
Prince Nadir's Secret Heir	Michelle Conder
Princess's Secret Baby	Carol Marinelli
The Renegade Billionaire	Rebecca Winters
The Playboy of Rome	Jennifer Faye
Reunited with Her Italian Ex	Lucy Gordon
Her Knight in the Outback	Nikki Logan
Baby Twins to Bind Them	Carol Marinelli
The Firefighter to Heal Her Heart	Annie O'Neil
Thirty Days to Win His Wife	Andrea Laurence
Her Forbidden Cowboy	Charlene Sands
The Blackstone Heir	Dani Wade
After Hours with Her Ex	Maureen Child

MEDICAL

Tortured by Her Touch	Dianne Drake
It Happened in Vegas	Amy Ruttan
The Family She Needs	Sue MacKay
A Father for Poppy	Abigail Gordon

MILLS & BOON®
Large Print – March 2015

ROMANCE

A Virgin for His Prize	Lucy Monroe
The Valquez Seduction	Melanie Milburne
Protecting the Desert Princess	Carol Marinelli
One Night with Morelli	Kim Lawrence
To Defy a Sheikh	Maisey Yates
The Russian's Acquisition	Dani Collins
The True King of Dahaar	Tara Pammi
The Twelve Dates of Christmas	Susan Meier
At the Chateau for Christmas	Rebecca Winters
A Very Special Holiday Gift	Barbara Hannay
A New Year Marriage Proposal	Kate Hardy

HISTORICAL

Darian Hunter: Duke of Desire	Carole Mortimer
Rescued by the Viscount	Anne Herries
The Rake's Bargain	Lucy Ashford
Unlaced by Candlelight	Various
The Warrior's Winter Bride	Denise Lynn

MEDICAL

A Secret Shared...	Marion Lennox
Flirting with the Doc of Her Dreams	Janice Lynn
The Doctor Who Made Her Love Again	Susan Carlisle
The Maverick Who Ruled Her Heart	Susan Carlisle
After One Forbidden Night...	Amber McKenzie
Dr Perfect on Her Doorstep	Lucy Clark

MILLS & BOON®
Hardback – April 2015

ROMANCE

The Billionaire's Bridal Bargain	Lynne Graham
At the Brazilian's Command	Susan Stephens
Carrying the Greek's Heir	Sharon Kendrick
The Sheikh's Princess Bride	Annie West
His Diamond of Convenience	Maisey Yates
Olivero's Outrageous Proposal	Kate Walker
The Italian's Deal for I Do	Jennifer Hayward
Virgin's Sweet Rebellion	Kate Hewitt
The Millionaire and the Maid	Michelle Douglas
Expecting the Earl's Baby	Jessica Gilmore
Best Man for the Bridesmaid	Jennifer Faye
It Started at a Wedding...	Kate Hardy
Just One Night?	Carol Marinelli
Meant-To-Be Family	Marion Lennox
The Soldier She Could Never Forget	Tina Beckett
The Doctor's Redemption	Susan Carlisle
Wanted: Parents for a Baby!	Laura Iding
His Perfect Bride?	Louisa Heaton
Twins on the Way	Janice Maynard
The Nanny Plan	Sarah M. Anderson

MILLS & BOON®
Large Print – April 2015

ROMANCE

Taken Over by the Billionaire	Miranda Lee
Christmas in Da Conti's Bed	Sharon Kendrick
His for Revenge	Caitlin Crews
A Rule Worth Breaking	Maggie Cox
What The Greek Wants Most	Maya Blake
The Magnate's Manifesto	Jennifer Hayward
To Claim His Heir by Christmas	Victoria Parker
Snowbound Surprise for the Billionaire	Michelle Douglas
Christmas Where They Belong	Marion Lennox
Meet Me Under the Mistletoe	Cara Colter
A Diamond in Her Stocking	Kandy Shepherd

HISTORICAL

Strangers at the Altar	Marguerite Kaye
Captured Countess	Ann Lethbridge
The Marquis's Awakening	Elizabeth Beacon
Innocent's Champion	Meriel Fuller
A Captain and a Rogue	Liz Tyner

MEDICAL

It Started with No Strings...	Kate Hardy
One More Night with Her Desert Prince...	Jennifer Taylor
Flirting with Dr Off-Limits	Robin Gianna
From Fling to Forever	Avril Tremayne
Dare She Date Again?	Amy Ruttan
The Surgeon's Christmas Wish	Annie O'Neil

MILLS & BOON®

Why shop at millsandboon.co.uk?

Each year, thousands of romance readers find their perfect read at millsandboon.co.uk. That's because we're passionate about bringing you the very best romantic fiction. Here are some of the advantages of shopping at www.millsandboon.co.uk:

* **Get new books first**—you'll be able to buy your favourite books one month before they hit the shops

* **Get exclusive discounts**—you'll also be able to buy our specially created monthly collections, with up to 50% off the RRP

* **Find your favourite authors**—latest news, interviews and new releases for all your favourite authors and series on our website, plus ideas for what to try next

* **Join in**—once you've bought your favourite books, don't forget to register with us to rate, review and join in the discussions

Visit **www.millsandboon.co.uk**
for all this and more today!